Katherine Rich was educated in London where she gained a BA in Fine Arts at London Guildhall University. Originally from Devon in England, she has been living and teaching in the UAE with her husband for several years, while indulging in her love of literature and writing. She has two children, James and Nadia. This is her first published novel.

For my children and my husband.

Katherine Rich

NIGHT CATCHERS

A Journey into Moonlight

AUSTIN MACAULEY PUBLISHERS™
LONDON · CAMBRIDGE · NEW YORK · SHARJAH

Copyright © Katherine Rich (2021)

The right of Katherine Rich to be identified as author of this work has been asserted by the author in accordance with Federal Law No. (7) of UAE, Year 2002, Concerning Copyrights and Neighboring Rights.

All rights reserved. No part of this publication may be reproduced, stored in a retrieval system, or transmitted in any form or by any means; electronic, mechanical, photocopying, recording, or otherwise, without the prior permission of the publishers.

Any person who commits any unauthorized act in relation to this publication may be liable to legal prosecution and civil claims for damages.

The age category suitable for the books' contents has been classified and defined in accordance to the Age Classification System issued by the National Media Council.

ISBN – 9789948258438 – (Paperback)
ISBN – 9789948258421 – (E book)

Application Number: MC-10-01-9400147
Age Classification: E

First Published (2021)
AUSTIN MACAULEY PUBLISHERS FZE
Sharjah Publishing City
P.O Box [519201]
Sharjah, UAE
www.austinmacauley.ae
+971 655 95 202

Bismillahir rahmanir rahim. Wa ladhikrullahi akbar. Writing is like magic, transporting us to other worlds but when one raises one's head from the page, there are people whose love and belief in what we do make everything possible. I would like to thank my husband for his relentless support, energy, and enthusiasm and my children and parents for their love, encouragement and belief. To Malcolm, who made all of these years successful and to my work colleagues and students for being inspirational. To Zahra, Alice and Esme who have been the best reading group I could have wished for and to Ahmed for putting up with me. Last but not least, to my brothers and sisters for the little things you do every day that make the world a better place.

I am coming soon Ayeeyo,
Listen for my skin and bones,
They always know where they came from.

For My Ayeeyo By Hamdi Mohamed

*

Flames sparked in the fireplace lending the room a warm glow while outside the winter wind snuck icy fingers through the curtains and underneath the doors. Dad and I had just had tea and I was reading my favorite adventure book when the doorbell rang. We were not expecting anyone and the weather was too terrible to leave the comfort and safety of home. There had just been an announcement on the radio. Storms and gales were forecast all across the country. Curiously I peered over Dad's shoulder as he answered to a man's voice.

"Come in, sir, no, no you are not intruding on our evening, we just finished dinner. This is my daughter Aya." Dad said, introducing me to the stranger.

With the opening of the door, the room had suddenly become cold and I shivered. A silver haired man in a designer suit walked over to where I sat and shook my hand.

"Hello, young lady." He spoke with a very English accent and his dark eyes smiled. I smiled back.

"You have your mother's eyes," he said unexpectedly.

I was caught off guard and looked at Dad for a moment. "You knew my mother?" I replied; startled.

"I worked with her a long time ago. A very clever and beautiful lady." He turned toward Dad. "I have never forgotten her, and that is why I am here. I am in a position to help your father. Is there somewhere we can talk?" he asked Dad.

"Without me hearing?" I said.

Dad rolled his eyes. "Aya, manners. Sorry Mr...."

"Mr Shah." He smiled offering a gloved hand.

After their secret meeting things were different. Dad said the meeting had not been so secret and that Mr Shah was trying to help the family, that he had a mutual acquaintance who knew Dad and they had talked about a perfect job at a London hospital and how it might suit us because it offered better prospects for our future.

And so, it was all set up and Dad was delighted. Everything was fine for a while. Well, when I say fine, I mean normal. That was before the strange behavior began. And when I say strange behavior I mostly mean singing. Yes, it was very worrying. Even more worrying was that he didn't even realize it was happening. There he was one evening cooking dinner and sort of humming a tune and smiling away over the chicken hotpot. Well, I should have guessed right there and then, but I didn't. The humming turned to singing and the singing turned into Jennifer.

It was almost a year ago, and I was thinking about it now as the train left London because after that, everything had changed.

The Move

Thunder shook the skies as the train pulled away from the platform at Kings Cross Station and rain pattered against its window panes like tears. The tall buildings of London's skyline gradually gave way to fields as me and Dad were swept away to another place, away from home, all we knew and all that was once familiar.

Imagine the life I used to live in the bustling, crazy, crowded city of London's metropolis. Buckingham Palace, Oxford Street, Big Ben, Hamleys, and my very best friends. Watching skateboarding on the Southbank of the Thames and boating in Hyde Park in all seasons. In short, it was the center of my universe and everything I knew and loved until Mr. Shah got Dad that new job and introduced him to Jennifer. Jennifer was perfect in every way, her elegant clothes and make up from Estee Lauder and Givenchy. Peeking at my crazy, ebony hair sticking out from underneath my hijab, mirrored in the window of the train, I took a deep, deep breath of my inhaler, and sighed.

And so, wedding bells had rung and now we were moving to the boggy Fens in Ely with its marshes and insects and, one particular boy, Joe, the most annoying of all, my step brother and committed foe. Being three years younger than me, our parents thought we'd get along swimmingly. Well, they were *so* very wrong. Every time we saw one another, a stare down ensued, spaghetti western style, emanating across the room, I'd narrow my eyes so that he knew we would always be arch enemies because he was everything I disliked about boys.

"Why, though, why do we have to be the ones to move?" I complained to Dad for weeks, groaning and throwing myself dramatically on cushions around the living room.

"*Habibti*, my beloved daughter," he answered patiently, "it will be alright, *inshallah* (god willing). You know that we are moving so that I can be a doctor in the countryside with Jennifer in our own practice. Together, a proper family. Mr. Shah, our beneficiary, has helped us and we must show gratitude. I know that once we move you will love your new life and Jennifer. You like her, don't you?"

"Yes," I said, "we get on perfectly." But what I couldn't say, what I had to hide, was 'she's not Mum!' And so was unable to reply honestly and after that concealing my feelings became normality. Shoulders back, gleaming eyes, he said, "Aren't you excited, just a little bit? Green trees, fields, fresh air. Reminds me of Africa. Living in the country will be good for you, much better for your asthma."

Defiantly I had replied, "I like the polluted air of London."

"Silly Aya," Dad said ruffling my hair and laughing.

He wasn't getting it, my diggy comments, little remarks. I could've screamed them from the rooftops. Nobody was listening.

Our arrival at the station came too soon. Jennifer was there waiting to pick us up that blustery day.

"Hey!" She waved at us in her anorak and wellies still managing to look elegant and glamorous. Looking down at my shoes, I knew they wouldn't do. Everyone at the station had wellingtons. It was the countryside after all. As if she knew what I was thinking, she hugged me and said, "Don't worry we'll get you some water proofs." We walked through the big old station and there he was, waiting on the bench, playing with a sling shot catapult. My nemesis, flicking peas at the birds. 'So childish.' We were to spend the whole summer holidays here before I started at a nearby boarding school for girls. It was going to be a very long summer.

"Joe, say hello to Aya." Jennifer was trying to coax us but it wasn't working.

His green eyes met mine as he raised the weapon above his short ginger hair. I gave him my special look, the one that says 'try it, just dare and see what will happen.'

As back seat prisoners forced into a cell together, we clambered reluctantly into the car. Boring lanes and Ely High Street flitted by not interesting me one jot. Neither did our arrival at the old Oat House where we were all being forced to live. Crumbling walls embraced an ancient building down a driveway covered in trailing ivy. On a nice day the bricks of limestone might have looked warm, but not today.

"Tea in the Theatre everyone?" Jennifer chirped merrily. Trudging through the house, I was taken on a tour like those your parents take you on when you're on holiday and you'd rather be on the beach but they decided you needed to learn about local history.

"We call it the theatre because, essentially, that's what it used to be. In olden days, two hundred years ago, the merchants and investors of the local Guilds would come to this huge old boardroom and, sitting around a big old table consider themselves extremely important. Stocks and shares would be sold, for crops and farmers in the agricultural trade. Later, my family added a stage in the 1920s and used to put on musicals and have fancy parties."

I tried to make my face look interested but I don't think it was working because Jennifer said, "Perhaps that's enough for now. Right, Joe will show you your room and me and your Dad will set up for tea. I've made cake, quiche, and sandwiches, and there's plenty of jam and cream."

Clever tactics, I thought, *using cake to bribe me*. I would not be bought. She was trying too hard.

Trudging reluctantly up the spiral staircase, I followed after Joe, who glared at me with eyes like steely furrows.

"Why do you wear that scarf on your head?" His rude question came.

"Because I'm Muslim," I declared, equally rudely.

"What's that?"

"Did you pay any attention at the wedding, Joe? It was a Muslim wedding after all."

"I was more interested in the food."

"Well, I can believe that. Islam is a religion and it means I believe in God."

"I know what religion is," he barked and at the same time made a kind of grunting noise that probably meant 'your room's in there,' and trudged off again leaving me furious. He was probably going off to kill things.

My room in the round spire had two small window views from its tower overlooking the garden North and West toward Ely Cathedral where the sun sets.

In all honesty, it was pretty like petals from blossom trees. Dad and Jennifer had moved most of my belongings in the weekend before. My little unicorn lay solemnly abandoned on the floor. Dad had hung a dream catcher in the window that he found in an old trunk of Mum's. Made by my grandmother, purple and silver feathers and beads sprinkled flecks of sunlight over my things. Picking up a photo of Mum and me when I was two, I flopped onto my bed like a sack of potatoes holding onto her.

Dad popped his head around the bedroom door. "Aya, come and join us. Jenny's serving your favorite, tea, sandwiches, and cakes."

I sighed. Why did I hate it so much?

Stormy, thunderous clouds threatened the afternoon as I joined the others in the Theatre room. Jennifer and Dad were laughing and Joe was waging a silent war across the table cloth with robots and soldiers around Jennifer's best china. Although it was summer, shadows sped across the walls.

"How is your room, Aya? Your dad said that your favorite color is lilac so we painted it for you. I hope you like it."

"Yes, thank you, I love it," I answered unenthusiastically. We sat there eating sandwiches, cake, and drinking tea, in perfect china cups painted with ancient ships and sails, quietly pretending everyone was happy. I gazed into them wishing myself away into another world.

And then a catastrophe took place, that probably, in a small way, changed fate; altering the course of my world and Joe's. For it was the reason we were sent to stay with Uncle Benedict.

Joe catapulted a soldier into my cake just as it reached my mouth, sending it flying onto my dress, splattering my face. I stood up, outraged.

"That's it!" I shouted banging my fists down onto the table. Reaching across to snatch the sling shot off an astonished looking Joe, I sent the china tea cups and teapot crashing to the floor shattering into a million pieces.

"Aya!" shouted Dad and Jennifer.

"What? It wasn't my fault!"

"That was my grandmother's tea set!" Jennifer cried out. The beautiful blue ships and porcelain white lay in shards on the floor.

"I don't care about your grandmother or her tea set. I don't want your especially made cake or your lilac room. What I do want is, my own house, my own room," and then I said it, the worst thing I could've said, "and my own mother!"

Nobody breathed, they just stared at me. I waited, face flushed red with rage. Joe knew, even being so young, even he knew how bad *I* was and the terrible thing I'd done. He looked from me to his mum and then to Dad. Jennifer was trying not to cry, I realized, starting to feel ashamed.

"Aya," Dad broke the silence, "go to your room." He'd never spoken to me before in that tone. I held my tears long enough to leave the Theatre before the damn burst.

Rain fell all that afternoon in dark drops of thundering disappointment. Downstairs, everything went on as normal, the chattering of voices, Joe pretending to be an airplane flying around the Theatre. Dad and Jennifer were clearing up dishes in the kitchen. They were all getting on with life without me in quiet harmony. I was no longer needed. I looked at the picture of my mother. "I didn't forget you," I said softly.

Lying on my bed and watching the sky rush by, I fell into a deep, strange sleep. Like many times before, an echoing voice whispered to me in my dreams. It had been this way since I was very little. I always tried to answer but my voice came only as a whisper. Below me was a red sea, I turned floating above it to a stairway in the cliffs and inside was a miniature universe. '*Aya,*' it called over and over again. I wanted to say '*Who is it? Who's there?*' But my voice was soundless and so a reply never came.

I woke suddenly in the early evening light, sitting bolt upright. "Dad?" I whispered. Outside, toward the Cathedral the sun was setting and the moon had risen low and large like a silver dish with Venus signaling beside it. Silhouettes of trees swayed in the evening breeze picking up dust into small swirls and creating tiny tornados. Shadows waited just outside the gate but the more I looked, the less they were there until I didn't know if I was dreaming or awake.

Sheepishly, walking into the kitchen, by now it was early evening, I sat at the table watching Dad cook a dinner of curried chicken.

"Are you feeling better?" he asked without turning around.

"Dad," I said. I wanted to tell him about the dreams, about the strangeness I felt, that something was calling me but how could I explain? So, I just said, "I'm hungry."

"Good," he said ending our conversation. He's never been big on words my Papa.

That night the wind howled ominously around my room in the spire and the dream catcher spun slowly to and fro as I slept but, out in the fens, something was calling. A soft lullaby echoed through my dreams, softly pulling me toward another world.

Helping Uncle Benedict

"Breakfast, Joe, Aya!" Dad shouted from the kitchen. Rubbing sleepy eyes and staring out into a bright, warm day, song birds chirped in the garden, inviting me to forget my restless sleep.

Nobody talked much as we ate. Everyone was trying to pretend that this might not be the biggest mistake of their lives. It was decided, not by me, that we would visit Jennifer's brother Benedict, since the sun seemed to have put in an appearance. Dad and Jennifer were shopping, *alone*. I couldn't argue, not since my performance yesterday which, I suspected, was at the bottom of it all and so I quietly relented.

We drove past fields of wheat and over level crossings, which I liked because of the danger that any moment a train might hurtle across causing a disaster that would making my own catastrophe with the crockery seem tiny and insignificant. Finally, at what seemed like the end of the world, across a rough track, surrounded by cherry, plum, and walnut trees, stood a bungalow in the middle of a field. Unlike an ordinary bungalow where people in the city lived, this one, painted eggshell blue, was more like a wooden beach hut from Looe or Dungeness and made me think of ice cream, beaches and summer holidays. As we pulled up, a shaggy black dog bounced down the drive to greet us, barking his hellos.

Sky, sky, and more sky, loomed high over flat marshland with high grasses and dark earth. I reached my hand out to grasp the clouds, but air fell through my fingers. Ely Cathedral sat in miniature on the distant horizon.

"He's an engineer," Dad had told me after breakfast.
"Like Mum," I said?
"Yes, like your mum."

This was the first interesting thing I'd heard since we'd arrived and I was just a little bit curious as we walked toward the house and strange noises whirred and buzzed mechanically from the direction of the shed. That is to say, they sounded like a creation was about to come alive.

"Buster, no, come back here, boy! Sit, stay!" his voice rang out from the house.

"Uncle Benedict!" Joe shouted scampering up the pathway.

"Joe, you scally wag, where is that catapult I made you?"

"Mum took it off me because Aya broke gran's china."

I groaned inside.

Uncle Benedict had gray hair that stuck up defying gravity. He wore glasses repaired with electrical tape, clothes covered in oil, and homemade sandals.

"You must be Aya," he said offering an oily hand. "Oh gosh," he said, "sorry!" Taking a rag from his pocket, he offered the newly wiped hand again. "I don't believe in shoes," he said catching me looking at his muddy toes. "And I make my own sandals. Shoes are the trappings of a capitalist society!"

"Benedict," Jennifer said, hugging her brother. *"You'll scare the children."*

"Oh yes, yes, of course, won't do at all, will it. Come on, Buster, let's show Aya around the grand estate."

He was joking, partly.

Dad had said that Uncle Benedict lived like a gentleman tramp and he was right. The bungalow walls were filled with old paintings and photos.

"That's my great grandfather, first world war, Max Buchanan." We stood in front of a faded painting of a young man with a moustache and serious eyes wearing an army uniform. "And that's the house in which I grew up, in Cambridge." He picked up a photo. We passed a painting of a young woman in a green dress with pretty round eyes and red hair. "My mother when she was a girl."

"You have a lot of memories from your family," I commented picking up a drawing of an outcrop of caves. The lines were unusual and must have been made as a study of geology and rock formations.

"Family is very important," he replied with a sideways glance. "It's where we come from, who we are."

Rugs from Iran and Turkey covered creaky old floorboards painted black. An oak desk, belonging to a once famous writer, overlooked an outcrop of trees and the garden meadow of wild grasses and flowers.

"My grandfather was an adventurer, back in the day. Travelled the Middle East, lived with Bedouin tribes in the desert. He didn't believe in shoes either, walked the entire Empty Quarter barefoot! Brought back many things but the greatest treasure of all was this necklace." He passed me, what looked like a giant ring of gold set with a shining emerald jewel shaped like a teardrop. It glimmered in the sunlight sparkling off the walls.

"It's rumored that it came from a mythical giant, once a prince who lost it in battle," he told me as I held it up to the sun and looked into it with one eye closed.

"It's like a magical treasure from Aladdin and the den of the Forty Thieves," I said turning it in my hand and letting the warm light of it cast soft shadows onto my skin.

"You can keep it if you like, one of the family now. Let's move on then!"

I didn't think it was a real emerald but it was very pretty. I smiled and put it in my pocket. "What's the Empty Quarter?" I asked.

"It's a place in the desert out in the far East where no one lives, too barren," he replied, "people wander through, adventurers, camel trains but it's very hot, turn the soles of your feet to leather!"

We moved into the small kitchen like the galley of a ship. Copper spoons and pans hung from the ceiling causing us to bump our heads. We crouched down low.

"Don't you have a cooker?" I asked, looking around.

"Why would I need one of those?" He screwed his nose up peering at me over his glasses, perplexed.

"Or a fridge?"

"Trappings! That's how they get you. And where does it start?"

"With shoes?" I replied cautiously.

"Exactly!" He seemed delighted with this answer. "You see, they tell us that we need all of these things but we don't really. It's their way of stopping you from being free, keeping you occupied, distracted, see?"

I didn't see and was going to ask who *they* were but thought it might be rude of me.

Half burned candles lay dotted around the room. "What about electricity? Is that a trapping too?" I enquired.

"Aha, good question, clever girl. I have something better than that, much better. I have a generator so I make my own. Self-sufficient, see? Come and look," he said briskly walking to the shed around the back garden. The big old generator, noisily chugging by the side of the house looked like something from another time when machines and engines were celebratory achievements. There were some odd bits of machinery too, set in the shape of an arch. Before I could ask about them, he marched me off to see his greenhouse leaning up against the bungalow wall where he grew tomatoes, red chilies, lettuces, and all sorts of delicious looking orange and yellow vegetables I hadn't seen before. Plastic bottles trailed from roof to floor in order to catch rain water and irrigate the plants.

"Fool proof, hardly ever have to water them myself."

I was impressed. Joe ran in just as I was going to ask about the other machine. "Can we go to the boat?" Jumping up and down, pulling at Uncle Benedict's sleeve. "Buster wants to go," said Joe.

"Aha, well then, if Buster insists then we can't disappoint!"

"You have a boat?" I said, looking around the fields.

"Ah, of course you've not been on the boat." Uncle Benedict winked at Joe, "Actually it's a special type, it's a Welsh Coracle."

We traipsed in line, Uncle Benedict, Buster, Joe, and I toward the riverbank hidden from sight. Tall golden grasses rippled softly in the breeze, hiding their secret pathways from us. Two planks had been laid over slippery mud, the reeds opened before me, and there she was. Lying low in the water, round as a full moon, the most beautiful little rowing boat ever seen. Her name was painted on the side. Buster leapt across the gangplank following Uncle Benedict and they were both swallowed up into the belly of *Moonlight*.

"Right, you two," Uncle Benedict said picking up some fishing rods, "you can earn your keep. If you want dinner, you'll have to catch it."

Spending the afternoon fishing on the river we watched its surface for signs of dinner, not even noticing that Dad and Jennifer had gone. Trout and eels were caught by Joe and I had a fish that I let go free. "Ahaa, the one that got away," Uncle Benedict cried marching us back into the kitchen to show us how to cook them. Running to the greenhouse to pick some herbs, we stuffed our catch and cooked it over the wood fired Arga. Joe picked fruit and nuts from the tree while Uncle Benedict dug up some potatoes. The afternoon light was golden by the time Dad and Jennifer had returned and we had enough food for a wonderful feast prepared entirely by us. When we reached home, we played a long game of Monopoly and drank hot chocolate.

Little did we know then, but as we slept that night, an ominous light glowed inside the shed releasing the whispering sounds of a million voices.

Entering the Other World

Suddenly I awoke. Beneath my slippers, I felt hot red dust. Quizzically, rubbing my eyes I thought, this is clearly not my room, not Ely, not even Earth! Good going Sherlock Holmes! Huge machine tracks gorged into the ground, that had me confused and dumfounded. Feeling unsafe, a sudden and desperate desire overcame me to escape. What was happening? "Dreaming, just dreaming, don't be stressed," I said trying to keep calm. It was like an episode of Dr Who, when the girl is transported through the universe in a time machine. I looked around me. Was there immediate danger? No. To the East, amber desert dunes rose high into the sky like soft, caramel mountains. Before me, lay an ocean of azure blue. Far away, on the horizon a volcano was erupting in violent flow, sending shards of hot magma into the night air. But more than this, towering in the sky above were two giant planets, Titans contained in clear cubes. One was blue like the oceans with small dots of green islands. The other was like Mars, dark and red with bursts of yellow fire. The two planets could not have been more different.

Curious now, I looked around. Pink mud houses lined the road trailing off into a maze of small alleyways. Warm winds caressed my face. My pajamas blew against my skin. I was wearing my pajamas! How embarrassing! I crept into the nearest alleyway, tiptoeing and peeping through a gate. An open backdoor to a house offered privacy and a place to hide until I knew how to deal with this very strange situation.

"Hello, Aya, I was wondering when you would arrive!"

An old woman stood at the kitchen counter, her back to me, making two cups of tea.

"Who are you?" I asked. "How do you know my name?"

"Do you know what the name Ayaanie means in Somalian legends? It means, an angel, a messenger between the Earth and the world of the Spirits."

With her kind African face, it's soft golden glow, she turned toward me in her dress of bright ochre cloth. Her graying hair poking out from under her loosely wrapped hijab. "Sit down, girl." She sipped her tea and looked closely at me. "I'm an interested party."

"What does that mean?" I asked, confused.

"It means that your mother is worried about you."

"Mum? Is she here?" My heart skipped a beat.

"No, no, she's not here, not in this place."

"Is she safe, is she OK? Did you see her?" Questions tumbled out of me.

"She would be if she wasn't worrying about you. Slow down, child."

I slumped back in my chair defeated. "What is this place, what is happening?"

"It is not the waking world, nor the dream but somewhere in between. It is a place made of moonlight," she smiled as she spoke.

"But it can't be, can it? How can that exist?"

"It exists and is as real as you or I."

"But you're not real!"

She frowned. "We're both here, aren't we, having a conversation? This is like your dream world, Aya, and right now it's very real. You can touch, you can hear, eat, and drink."

Right then I realized that I was tasting my tea.

"In this world, everything you experience is real. You can walk around it, you can decide what happens but you must be clever, you must use your power, Aya, or you are in danger."

"Danger of what?"

Right at that moment a siren sounded loudly and with urgency. She looked worried. "I can help you but right now we have to get you away from here. They are coming. You are not safe. Quickly, follow me, they have come too soon. She took my hand and we ran through the back door, down some steps and into a basement. A hidden door in the wall opened up."

"You must find the Tomb of Qelhatat in Sector B. Tell them that Fatima sent you and that will earn their trust. Quickly, girl, run, run for your life. They are coming for you and will not stop."

"But..." the door closed and she was gone. "Are you Fatima?" I shouted into empty space.

Sector A and the Castle of Huur

Sharp eagle eyes surveyed the room. Stripes of gold and blue sparkled from his robes and crown as he sat back on his dark carved throne. Even seated, he rose meters above everyone else in the System, that is, apart from the giants Habbad ina Kammas and Biriir ina Barqo. He had sensed my arrival and was not amused that I had slipped through his clutches.

"And so, you are telling me you have lost her?" a voice like metal, cruel and cold echoed across the vast temple hall.

"We will find her your majesty. We know that she arrived in Sector C. She is certain to return and we will capture her then."

Huur sat forward leaning menacingly with narrowed eyes. "Oh, indeed you will find her, because if you do not then you will be sent to the dungeons." He tightened his fist crushing the steel cane beneath his grip. "Where is the woman?"

"Sire, she is here," he gestured for Fatima to be brought forward where she stood gracefully and upright before him.

Angered by her lack of fear, Huur rose from his throne and began pacing around her. "So, you will not speak?"

Fatima raised her eyes. "I am not afraid of you, Huur. The girl will bring you down even if I am not there to witness it. You cannot continue to destroy our world."

A deafening screech pierced through the temple walls. "You dare to question my authority? This world does not belong to you. I own it and I can save it or destroy it as I choose."

Fatima sighed. "You would drown it, Huur, you would poison it. Don't think I don't know what you started, all those years ago."

Rage grew in Huur like spiders crawling through his veins. "I will send the Jinn for the girl and you will learn your place and understand who is the Master."

Before Fatima was taken away she turned back to look at Huur straight in the eye and say, "We will defeat you, Huur, let there be no doubt."

A man entered from behind Huur gazing at the spot where Fatima had left.

"You heard everything?" Huur asked

"Yes. She knows nothing and anyway it is too late. Our plans have been long in the making, The Gate is open and the delivery is on its way. We have already dispatched the next consignment."

Huur replied, "The Jinn have been sent. There is no escape for the girl."

Deep within the Pyramid, a large Cube known as the System watched all the events unfold, its silent eye scanning the Sectors seeing everything. A million cubes saw the people, a million cubes directed and distracted. When something occurred that was not permitted, the System dealt with it and fed back information to Huur. He was the Master, after all. It was his great achievement and meant that nothing that happened could do so without his knowledge.

After the visitor had gone, Huur stood in front of this room, with the Cube rising up before him. It was where he felt most at peace. Each person connected to a Cube was his. There were some that had escaped him but eventually he would have them all, one way or another.

Over the city of pyramids that stretched into the distance like a mountain range and rose up as high toward the sky, chilling cries rang out across the landscape as a machine reared its metal limbs and opened mechanical eyes but there was something else too, a shadow, something not quite human. A veil of darkness had awoken.

Yielding to the Machine

When I looked back for the house, it had disappeared. Just like that in a plume of smoke, leaving me standing in a bustling market street alone. It was beautiful and old like the medieval towns from Africa that I had seen in Papa's photos. There were colorful woven fabrics of ochre yellow and deep purple being sold in the market square. Fruits, spices, and flowers of strange colors and shapes sat in carts being purchased by people from many different places. Plumes of smoke mingled with food cooked on fires drifting over the square, sending aromas of delicious cooking my way, making me hungry. Something about it felt familiar. *I remember this*, reaching out my hand to touch it. *Long ago, when I was young, a child, we came here, didn't we?* My head was all fuzzy and confused. I was still wondering about Fatima and what she had said about my mother and the Tomb of Qelhatat. Remembering that this was a dream, and Fatima said it was real, I thought I should investigate.

Next to me, in the busy street stood a screen on a pillar with a map. Puzzling over it, it informed me that I was on Sector C and that the planets above me were Sectors A and B. Hadn't Fatima said something about getting to the Tomb of Qelhatat on Sector B? All around, people rushed by. I wondered why, and if they could see me. When they slowed down it was clear that each one had a Cube attached to their forehead. They seem to be communicating, distracted by it. It made me think of people on their mobile phones walking down the streets oblivious to everyone else.

On the horizon a storm of dust was being whipped up and white tumultuous clouds worked their way with ever increasing speed across the landscape toward me. *Time to go*, I thought.

Rushing faster away from the oncoming storm, pushing, jostling swarms of people began moving in crowds around me. More and more people rushed past at ever-increasing speed, not realizing I was there when suddenly, he appeared with one of those screens in front of his eyes, and, not looking, we collided with a crash. His arms had been full of large fruits that smelt like blueberries.

For a moment I lay stunned, on the floor. He peered down, lifting his cube away from his eyes.

"Oh no, I'm so sorry!" He offered a hand to help me up.

"Idiot!" I shouted taking my inhaler out of my pocket. "Watch where you are going!" The boy who stood before me was about my age. I thought he might be from Pakistan or India if we were on Earth. He had large brown eyes and a slight curl to his shiny black hair. His ears were quite large but so was his friendly smile.

"Kareem," he smiled, "male, fourteen years old, C minor. Do you want help or are you just going to sit there?"

I accepted his hand, brushing the dust off my pajama's. "Aya, 13, the Earth, major or minor depending who you ask," I replied sarcastically.

"What is that?" he indicated as I took my inhaler out of my pocket. The air was dusty from the fall.

"It's an inhaler, for my asthma. Haven't you seen one before?" I questioned thinking that a bit strange.

"No, that!" He said pointing to the Monopoly money bundle I had won from the game, which had fallen out of my pocket.

"I've never seen that amount of money before. How'd you get it?" His questioned seemed real. He narrowed his eyes and, frowning he said looking at my dressing gown, "You are dressed very strangely."

"Well, well," I blustered, "you have a cube on your head!"

"I do," he replied, "where is your cube?"

"I don't have one, silly."

A concerned look came over him and he turned toward the dust storm. The Cube that belonged to Kareem spoke, "In all probability, the girl has been detected."

"Agreed, Cube," Kareem replied and then to me he said, "you can't stay here, I can help if you give me some of that cash."

I looked down at the Monopoly money. "It's a deal," I replied.

"Right then, follow me." He rushed off as he spoke and I could barely keep up pace. The Cube directed us.

"Wait," I shouted, "who is coming? What do you mean? Am I in danger? Is that storm coming for me?" I followed Kareem quickly through the streets of pink sand walls, through a maze of alleys and pathways. My slippers now covered in red dust. By the time we stopped I was a little breathless and exasperated. An ancient doorway in the wall led us into a small open courtyard of palms and water fountains and tiles painted a beautiful blue with Arabic designs. It was cool and peaceful under palm trees and soft shafts of light.

We sat on floor cushions. It was soothing and pretty.

"So, tell me," he enquired. "What is going on?"

"I don't know, I just appeared here and then Fatima said to find the Tomb of Qelhatat."

Kareem consulted his cube. "Fatima, 71 years old, C Major, missing, presumed enemy."

"What? Enemy of who?"

"Of Huur, the ruler of The System. Oh dear, without your Cube, how could you possibly know, well, anything? You must feel very sad and lonely."

"I'm not," I protested, "either of those things."

"Then why are you here without your Cube?"

"I don't know," came my curt reply.

The Cube lit up. "My lying indicator predicts that you are, in all probability, telling the truth.

"Let's see if we can help you out before they arrest you and take you to the dungeon." Kareem tried to smile reassuringly but without success.

"The girl's fear indicators have risen," said the Cube.

I narrowed my eyes and stared at it. "Just tell me a few simple things please because I'm a bit lost and confused. What is that cube thingy on your head?"

"This connects to The System, and Huur is the Supreme Ruler."

"What is it for?"

"You don't know much, do you?"

I give him my special reserved look for boys and said "Please, just answer the question."

"It's a central computer so that you can play the game and earn levels. Its where we get all our information and instructions from. Anyway, it's mandatory."

"Who says?"

"Huur, jeez weez!"

"OK, what year is it?"

"Ah we don't have that here," Kareem replied.

"Don't have what?"

"Time, linear time. I've heard of it, the thing you are talking about but it's got no use."

"How can time have no use?"

"It doesn't make any sense, does it? Think about it. How old is time?"

"Nobody knows that, silly," I replied.

"My point exactly. Time is not measurable in any useful sense, therefore it has no use."

"So, how do you measure things?"

"By levels. Every level takes as long as it needs to."

I thought for a moment. "What about History then?"

"History—something that tells us about people's past," the Cube said.

"It's like layers. You've played computer games, right?"

"Sort of."

"Well, then, the computer generates a game and people come in at different stages. It's like that but the game is the entire universe and is ruled by The System."

"And Huur," I replied.

"Exactly," said Kareem.

It was a lot to take in. "Fatima said that I was lucid dreaming. Does that mean that you are too?"

"Sort of. You're a visitor but I'm a permanent resident." He tapped his Cube again.

"Oh, I see! But that means you can't leave?"

"Why would I want to leave? I'm only on level 27500."

"So, what is the point of the game?" I asked.

"Cube, what is the point of the game?" Kareem asked.

"Does not compute, Kareem. The System exists, therefore the game exists."

The floor began to shake and the walls shudder. Sirens filled the air and far away, a distant boom. Something was coming, something very big.

"Kareem," Cube said calmly, "I believe Habbad ina Kamas is coming."

"Oh, not good. Let's get going." Kareem pulled at my arm but I had to see.

The shaking grew louder as it approached rumbling like an earthquake. I walked to the door, gazing up into the sky and saw it. An enormous, gargantuan machine larger than the highest building I had ever seen, was coming for me. I was transfixed. It looked like one of Joe's toy robots but a hundred-fold bigger with large eyes and a block like body. But this one had a giant Cube. Its arm contained a laser chamber and it was primed and ready, advancing quickly. Then it stopped, turned its large block head and looked directly at me. As soon as it detected me, it fired. It was not joking either. Everything around me exploded and wood splintered through the air.

"I think we should leave now," Kareem shouted. We turned and bolted through the back of the garden through neat, cool rooms, back through the kitchen door and out into the alley mazes. We sprinted a myriad of turns until I didn't know which direction we were running, but still it powered on after us, trampling everything in its path. Boom, boom, boom, it fired again and only missed us by an inch as we ducked under an archway. We couldn't lose it. It tracked us relentlessly and I was tiring fast. Then I noticed the glow of its Cube.

"Turn off your Cube!" I shouted to Kareem.

"It's helping us," he yelled back breathlessly, still running.

"It's tracking us. If you don't turn it off, we are going to die!"

"You are losing levels. Danger of losing a life. The girl is correct," said the Cube.

We rounded a corner and for a moment seemed to lose it. Crouching low behind a staircase Kareem said, "Yes, it's using sat nav. Cube, shut down navigation."

The screen flashed. It said in its monotone computer voice. You may lose your level status.

"Do it anyway."

"Alright, Kareem, shutting down navigation."

We sat there in silence, crouching in the shadows. The giant stood bolt upright. "He must have been sensing we had gone offline." Kareem spoke softly. For a moment, it stood still. Then, without warning it turned completely and walked away in the direction it had come.

"You have gained a level," Cube said ironically.

"Thanks, Cube, that's incredibly useful information." My comment was a little bit sarcastic. Breathing a sigh of relief, we rested, backs against the wall.

"What was that?" I panted.

"That's Habbad ina Kamas and he's not known for his friendliness. He is an agent of Huur, the Ruler of the System. He takes people to him, and they are never seen again. Why are they so interested in you?"

"I have no idea. Right now I'm just trying to find my mum. Fatima said something about finding the Tomb of Qelhatat."

"Ahhh, that is a long, long way away."

"How long?"

"Kareem looked into the sky and pointed to the largest of the planets."

"How do we get there?" I asked.

"*We*, don't get there," he said, tucking the wad of toy money into his pocket that I'd just handed over. "Nobody gets to Sector B."

I trudged after him as he walked down the street the way we had come. "Oh come on," I said, "nothing is impossible."

"Not true," he replied. "Some things are definitely impossible, like flying with no wings, drinking through your eyeballs and, oh yeah, getting to Sector B."

"You can get me there." I was challenging him. "You know how to get through the levels."

"Yeah, about that, I'm really busy just now trying to complete level 275002."

Suddenly, up ahead a village appeared like a mirage. "Where did that come from?" I said. "I swear that wasn't there a moment ago."

"Landscapes appear. It's the levels. If you complete a level you move on to the next."

As if hearing us, Cube spoke. "Level 276003."

"That's odd," Kareem said. "There must be something wrong. Cube, assess faulty data."

"There is no faulty data, Kareem," Cube replied.

"What's wrong?" I asked

"Well, the levels are supposed to go up one at a time but my level has just risen by one thousand," he answered perplexed.

We crouched down behind some bushes to assess danger of detection from the villagers. Everyone had Cubes and it was possible that our not-so-friendly giant was still within firing distance and might be alerted to our presence. It was lively and bustling with people whose Cubes shone brightly. Galloping across the savannah were animals that looked like horses.

"Unique Horns!" Kareem said.

"Unicorns!" I replied

"No, no, these are Unique Horns, named because of their antennae. It makes each of them individual and allows them to pick up information with their aerial. Animals don't have

Cubes. They have their own transmission systems and so self-regulate."

"They are not controlled by Huur?"

"No, he can't track them but he has no interest in them. They help the villagers and are kept and fed by them."

There were Unique Horns carrying water between huts on stilts, ferrying people with crops and sacks. They all looked very contented apart from one young Unique Horn close by between the village and where we were hiding.

"What's wrong with that one?" I asked Kareem. "It looks sad."

"It's the wrong color. The others have rejected it. It'll need to look after itself."

I was horrified, "What do you mean? They've thrown it out?"

"Yup, it's all wrong, see the tint of lilac in its coat? It should be pure silver like the others.

When an animal has given up, you can sort of tell. There's something in its eyes, from its soul.

"Well, I'm not leaving it!"

"No," Kareem called out in a loud whisper as I crouched down and sped off toward the abandoned Unique Horn. I could hear him shuffling about awkwardly and sighing behind me. Still unobserved, I knelt down beside it and stroked its purple coat.

"Hello there, I'm Aya, what's your name?" It was silent but seemed to like me and gazed up with sad eyes. After a while of gentle coaxing, I convinced it to stand up and we hurried back to Kareem.

"Look," I said, "if you can get me to Sector B, the rest of this is yours." I held out the rest of the Monopoly money.

"Phew, that's a lot of dosh." I could see he was weighing everything up carefully.

"And there's more where that came from," I replied confidently.

"I can't promise anything but I'll do my best," he nodded. "Now, we need to get away from here before we're discovered," he said. "Is it coming with us?"

35

For a moment, the *it* stood mournfully, looking back at the village. Then it buried its nose into my shoulder and snuffled.

"Come on my friend," I said in reply. "Let's go. I will call you Faras,".

"Erm, have you got experience in riding one of these?"

"A little," I lied.

"Cube, calculate the percentage of truth in that answer," Kareem said frowning as we galloped off together toward the horizon.

Above us in the vast skies, on Sector A, an electrical pulse flashed on and off, on and off.

Signs

Jennifer sat at the end of my bed the next morning holding a cup of tea.

"Wakey, wakey, sleepy head," she said, brightly.

"Morning. What time is it? I was dreaming, really dreaming," I answered propping myself up on my pillows. It was not easy being in one place and then suddenly in another and I felt more than a bit disorientated. But the tea helped. It was nice and sweet. We sat in silence for a while. "I'm sorry, about the tea set. I don't think I apologized properly."

"It's just a tea set," she sighed with resignation.

"But it was your grandmother's. It must have been special to you."

"People are more important than things, Aya," she said in reply and I was grateful.

We sat in silence for a moment longer before Jennifer spoke again. "It's a nice day, what would you like to do?"

I appreciated that she had changed the subject and felt a little forgiven. "Can we visit uncle Benedict again? I need to see what he's doing in that workshop."

Jennifer smiled. "That sounds like a plan. I'll tell Joe, he'll be delighted."

I waited until Jennifer left before groaning and falling back onto my pillow.

Uncle Benedict was busy when we arrived. He lifted his goggles and wiped his oily hands on a cloth but continued on with his work. Joe and Buster ran through to the back garden. He had been complaining all the way in the car that his robot had gone missing and Dad was saying he'd probably left it at Uncle Benedict's so he and Buster went looking for it.

I watched curiously as Uncle Benedict worked. "What is it?" I asked.

"Hard to describe," he replied. I waited for more information but none was forthcoming so I continued. "It looks like a kind of gate."

"A gate, good description, that's sort of what it is."

"A gate for what?"

"Or, for where?" came his mysterious reply.

I watched the horses running in the field beside Uncle Benedict's land and whispered, "Just like the Unique Horn."

He stopped still in his tracks. "What did you say?" he asked.

"A Unique Horn is a kind of horse but with…"

"Its own personal antennae," he replied. "I know what a Unique Horn is. The million-dollar question is, how do you know about it?"

We sat down in the workshop as I recounted my dream and although it wasn't the first one, they had been getting much stronger recently and more vivid.

"Well I am astounded. I was expecting something," he said, "all these years I've waited! There are few who have the ability to move between the two worlds. The ability to journey into Moonlight. No one knows why some are chosen and some cannot enter. Perhaps you are being called for a purpose."

Now I was beginning to get very excited. "Fatima said that my name meant Ayaanie—an angel between the Earth and the world of the Spirits."

"I don't think your name is an accident, Aya."

"But my, mother gave me my name. Papa always talks about it. It is a tradition passed down amongst the women from our tribe."

"Well, I think there is a reason behind it, that you would have the power to act as a messenger."

"So Fatima was right, it's a real place then, Moonlight?"

"As real as you or I."

"And, you've been there?" I whispered reverently.

"Yes, many years ago. I've been trying to get back ever since. This is what all this is for." He gestured around the shed.

"But how? If you were not called into the world...." and then I realized. "The gate," I said, "it's to link the worlds, isn't it? For those who can't enter in their sleep?"

"Yes. There may be others like you, Aya, that have this gift and are not aware of it. But for people like me a Gateway is the only way in and out so that those who are trapped can come back freely."

"Are they trapped?"

"Some, perhaps like your mother."

"And you believe that my mother is there, truly?"

"Fatima believed it, perhaps she even knows."

"I need to go back, I need to find her."

"You must not get caught. You've been very lucky so far but that may not last. Look for signs that will guide you."

"What do you mean?"

"Things will appear from this world in the other and vice versa."

"What things? How do I know what to look for?"

"You have to trust your intuition. Sometimes, they are obvious, other times less so. And, Aya, if Huur finds you, you could be trapped forever. Now tell me, have you lost anything recently, has anything gone missing in this world?"

Just then Joe appeared at the doorway. "Uncle Benedict, have you seen my robot?"

To Find a Cave

Uncle Benedict suggested that in order to return to the same point in time, I should concentrate hard when going to sleep. It was not easy. Have you ever tried to think clearly and fall asleep at the same time? It's a contradiction. I thought about the last time I was with Kareem and Faras, and slowly drifted into sleep. At first, I dreamt of giant ice creams chasing me down Ely High Street. Next, I was on a boat and the wind started to blow me away from the shore but on the third attempt, I was back there and Kareem and I were galloping through Moonlight on Faras. He seemed to not notice that I'd been gone.

"Level 277004," announced Cube.

Up ahead lay a group of tumbling ruins. Some were free standing and the color of the red desert sand. We dismounted. The place appeared to be deserted. Cautiously, we walked around the free-standing pillars rising above us. The stone had been intricately carved with high arches tumbling in decay.

"An ancient city?" I said.

"They are certainly very interesting. Cube, what is this place?"

"The ruins of Adal Sultanate, once part of a great empire. All other information has been erased."

"So you do have History, it's just not been recorded."

Kareem was confused and a little put out. "Why is there no information on this place? Clearly it existed and people have been here, an ancient people."

We wandered underneath a high arched doorway into a cool dark chamber.

"What happened here?" I asked. "Why has the information been erased?"

"If Huur created The System on this planet, there must've been something before Huur?"

"True, but nobody knows what that was. There are stories, legends about the world having its own name but The System replaced everything."

"But its name is Moonlight, isn't it?" I asked.

"How do you know, that? I've always known it as the System," Kareem replied.

"Because Huur wiped away History," I gasped. "He erased the name!"

"I guess," replied Kareem coolly.

"Don't you care, Kareem, about your heritage, your History?"

Kareem shrugged. "It's all I know, it's a game. I enjoy playing the levels."

"What about *your* history, do you have one?"

"Of course, everyone on Earth has a history. It's important in telling us who we are?" Then I realized that I didn't really know much about my history at all until Fatima told me about my name.

I changed the subject, "So, what level am I on?"

"Technically," Kareem replied, "you only become part of the game if you are in The System."

"So if I get captured what happens?"

"They will probably send you for processing but can't say for definite."

"Don't you remember when you arrived?"

"I remember everything after but nothing before."

"Kareem, how long have you been here?"

"What a daft question. I've always been here."

"But have you? Where are your parents, your family?"

"The System is my family."

"No, you must have come from somewhere. I mean, I come from Earth right and we are here together. So, you must originate, belong somewhere."

"I guess. It's just, the System is all I remember."

Inside the chamber our eyes began to adjust to the light. Carved out rooms seemed to watch us with hollow eyes.

Windchimes hung from the ceiling moving softly from an unseen breeze.

"I think this is a sign," I said to Kareem. "Come on."

"What do you mean, sign?"

"Like a map, like breadcrumbs, Uncle Benedict told me about them and Fatima. There is a way through this world, Kareem, and we need to find it."

We pushed forward along the path until we came to a staircase carved from stone. A strange light radiated on the ceiling. "Shall we look?" I asked curiously.

"Err, I don't think we should," Kareem turned as if to leave.

"Oh, come on, Kareem, don't you want to know what's down there?"

"No, I'm good."

"I'm going, you wait here with Faras."

Kareem frowned at the Unique Horn. "I don't think it likes me."

"Of course, it likes you. Faras, look after Kareem."

Faras shuddered and stomped her front hoof.

Stepping softly down the stairs, my hands brushing against the cool walls as they spiraled downward, I was nervous. I stopped. A soft sobbing noise was coming from below. Tiptoeing, I peered around the corner, seeing an iridescent light filling the lower staircase. The sobbing echoed ominously around a cave in the half light. The vast cavern, filled with a strange blue lake, was empty. So why did I think I'd been listening to Joe?

At the top of the stairs the Cube lit up. "Level 300,000."

"What? That's impossible!" Kareem said, astonished.

Engineering a Gate

Early in the morning, Dad and I prayed Fajr prayers facing towards Mecca. We sat on cushions looking up at the night stars through the window, before dawn.

"Dad?"

"Yes, *habibti*?"

"Have you ever heard of the Tomb of Qelhatat?"

He looked at me in surprise. "Where did you hear about that?"

"Erm just around."

"It is an important place for women, an ancient place in Somalia where Queen Qelhatat rests. She was a great warrior and tribal leader. It is said that the Queen of Sheba sent her gold and many gifts, but those are myths, ancient stories, many of which are lost."

I thought about it for a while. "What would this place be like, Dad, if I were to go there?"

"You would be immersed in the underworld, where the earth and ocean exist together. It is said that the warriors can breathe underwater and that their friends are the animals and creatures of the sea."

"Tell me what Mum was like." We used to do this when I was younger, talk about her. Dad would take the photo out of me and Mum, sit me curled up next to him, and tell me stories. But it had been a long time since we had done this.

"She was the wisest woman with a strong heart and mind. Everyone in the village went to her for advice. She could be trusted. Her hair was as dark as the night and her limbs like the roots of a tree, strong and smooth. When she smiled the birds sang and the cheetah ran alongside her but when she raged the earth shook."

I smiled at this image of her. "And Somalia?"

"You don't remember? Ah, you were so small when we took you there. The stars were so bright at night, you could see the whole sky and the animals were like our friends. It's not how it is here with pets, animals help you in Somalia, you work side by side. In the summer the plains stretch for hundreds of miles towards the mountains. You could walk for days without seeing a single person, only trees, and when the monsoons came, there were many rivers that brought life to the people and to the land."

"I would like to see it. Why can't we go, Papa, why not go back?"

"My Ayaanie, in times of war, there is so much pain. Sometimes it is better to look forward than to try to find lost happiness."

At the breakfast table I sat chomping hungrily on toast and marmite thinking about the cave. I finished my orange juice, wiped my mouth clean with the back of my hand, and stared at Joe.

"How are you?" I asked. I was looking for signs. Joe eyed me suspiciously.

"Fine," he replied, "what about you?"

Jennifer and Dad exchanged glances, raising their eyebrows.

Joe jumped up and ran into the garden. I followed. "Sleep OK?" I asked.

"Yup," came the hasty reply. He'd found a stick and was beating the hedge with it.

I eyed him suspiciously. Cautiously, I said, "I miss my mum."

Joe frowned and sat on the grass. "I don't see my dad much."

"How come?"

"He has another family. I used to see him a lot when, you know, my parents split but then he had another family and we don't really see him now." We were both quiet for a while watching the sparrows dive and swoop around the garden. Joe squinted and looked over at me. "Mum said that your mum died."

"Yes, she died of cancer when I was two years old."

"Do you remember her, you know, what she looked like?"

"Only from photos."

"I've forgotten what my dad sounds like," Joe said sadly.

At that moment a galloping sound came from the driveway and there, looking very purple and out of place, stood my beloved unicorn Faras. Something was happening. I didn't know if it was good or bad but I knew that we needed to get to Uncle Benedict's, and fast.

Before Dad and Jennifer could discover that there was a Unicorn in the back garden, I rushed into the kitchen, grabbed some apples and said, "Uncle Benedicts here, don't need to take us, me and Jo are off, be back later, bye," and dashed out the door. "Come on, Joe, let's go."

"Where are we going?" Jo asked in surprise.

"I'll explain on the way, trust me." I held out my hand to him which he eyed suspiciously and then took. There was only one way that something as large as Faras could've come through from the other world, and if Faras came through, what else might?

By the time we got there, Uncle Benedict was gone. The doors to the shed were thrown wide open and we could hear a humming sound. Peeping in, I knew that the Gate was alive. It was glowing. We stood side by side.

"I know what you're thinking," Joe said, "if we go in there, we go in together." I nodded in agreement.

"Oh crikey!" I cried as we stepped forward into the hum of the gate. "Your mum's going to kill me!"

Making Discoveries in the Emerald Jungle

Kareem was sitting by the underground lake when we arrived. "Something is happening," he said without looking up, something serious. "My levels are behaving erratically and now Cube has shut down."

"That's just great," I replied. "Uncle Benedict is mixed up in this, I can feel it. He never said what happened the last time he was here but he's waited a long time to return. Joe, this is Kareem, Kareem this is Joe, my sort of brother."

Suddenly, behind us the Gate slammed closed and the stairway disappeared. We were locked inside the cave with no obvious exit.

"The Gate, no! It's gone." Joe beat his hands against the wall shouting, "Help, let us out!"

"Look, Joe," I spoke calmly though I didn't feel it, "there must be a way out or Uncle Benedict would still be here. We can't be too far behind him."

"The cavern is changing," said Kareem. "We must be moving through another level."

We looked around the huge cave. It felt as though the world was spinning. Faras lit up her horn which emitted a golden glow. All around us on the ceiling and cave walls were painted figures and animals, some depicted hunters and horses painted in orange and deep red pigments but others were of wild fantastical creatures described using strange writing that looked like hieroglyphs from ancient Egypt.

"Who do you think did those?" Joe asked nervously.

"I don't know, ancient people, thousands of years ago. I very much doubt they are still here," I replied looking around hoping I was right. "Over there," I pointed. "Look!"

Kareem said, "It looks like a boat but it's too far, we can't get to it. Can anyone swim?"

We eyed the water with suspicion but our hero Faras waded straight in and began swimming to the other side of the cave, her glowing light ebbing further away until almost out of sight. We waited. After a long anxious while, Faras returned towing the small rowing boat. She held the rope in her teeth.

"Faras, you are a marvel." I gave her a huge hug as she shook water all over us.

"Let's go," said Kareem. "Joe sit in the front, Aya, can you row?"

"Yes, Uncle Benedict taught me."

The boat slipped eerily through the strange blue water, with Faras swimming alongside.

"How far do you think it goes back?" asked Joe.

"No need to be scared, Joe, we've got you," comforted Kareem.

"I'm not scared. I can attack anything that might come for us," he said taking aim with his catapult. "I brought extra shot just in case."

"You can be our look out." I smiled. I could tell that Joe was trying to be brave.

As we rowed through the cavernous space, we started to see blue and white objects floating in the water and then I noticed that Faras was shaking off something from her horn.

"Plastic bags! Where would plastic come from in this world?" I turned to ask Kareem.

"This is a very strange material," he said. "I've never seen it before. It looks dangerous."

Joe explained what plastic was to Kareem and he was not impressed.

"So it lasts forever?"

"It takes a long time to break down and can be very dangerous to wildlife," I said. "We learnt that at school."

"Why would anyone produce a material that did that?" Kareem asked.

Nobody could answer. To say that we needed bags to carry shopping home seemed like a silly answer given what we had just told him.

At the far side of the cave, the chamber roof lowered, funnelling us into a narrow channel faster and faster until we could no longer row but only pull the oars in and hold on tight to the side of the boat propelled by the fast current. Faras was struggling to swim and for a few moments was left behind us as we raced toward an eerie green light.

The cave spewed us out into a vast jungle where the river widened and the trees blocked out the sun. Large winged birds cried and circled high in the treetops and the light only reached us in shafts. Dust motes flitted in the half light.

"Wow, this is like Jurassic Park," Joe said, awestruck.

The river widened and slowed as we rowed toward the mud bank, anxiously looking back for Faras.

Suddenly, bursting up from the river bubbled Faras, sneezing water from her snout and shaking out her mane. We all laughed and felt a pang of relief.

Cube turned itself back on and announced us to be on level 350,000.

"This has never happened before," said Kareem, fiddling with Cube's functions.

"What a strange place," I whispered. Everything seemed so big and apart from the bird cries, the trees were filled with was a strange stillness. "Shall we continue by boat or walk?"

"The forest looks impenetrable," replied Kareem looking around. Rubbish and plastic littered the ground covering everything.

"Why is there so much rubbish here?" Joe asked. "It looks like it's been here for years."

"I don't know, Joe, but I don't like it one jot. I think we need to get out of this place," I replied glancing around with concern.

A digital noise announced Cube's return. "Hello, Kareem, it's good to see you again."

"Thanks, Cube. I need to know where we are."

"You are in the Emerald Jungle. It is one of the oldest ever recorded."

"Don't tell me, there is no information about it since Huur took power, correct?"

"Correct," replied Cube. "Although there is something useful that looks as though it was added recently."

"Well, that's good news, what is it?" asked Kareem.

"The Emerald Jungle is almost certainly inhabited by a mythical demon named Dhegdheer. She is cannibalistic and likes to eat lost children," the Cube said in a matter of fact way. "Also, the jungle has been dying for the past decade."

"Are you joking me?"

"I do not joke, Kareem, you know that. In all probability I am 99.8 percent correct in my information."

We all looked at one another.

"We need a way out of here. Cube, can you direct us?"

"There is no known path out of the Emerald Jungle..." Just then, far in the distance, the thunderous earth shook. Kareem silenced Cube by shutting it off mid-sentence. We stood still silently and listened.

"Habbad ina Kamas?" I questioned.

"Could be," said Kareem.

"What do you think Cube meant by 'no known path' out of the jungle?" asked Joe.

"I'm not sure, Joe. Maybe it's just a difficult level."

"But you can get us out, right? You're on level 200 million or something," Joe asked hopefully.

Kareem tried his reassuring look. "There is always a way out. Let's try a path along the river," came Kareem's reply. "Come on, let's move. I don't like the sound of that Dhegdheer."

We rowed on until thick, slimy plant roots and plastic clogged the river, slowing our progress so that we had to drag the boat onto soft, muddy marsh and trudge by foot. Plastic and metal seemed to be corroding and suffocating plants at their roots. Fading light echoed menacing noises through the trees and I had the terrible feeling we were being watched. I'd stop suddenly to listen for footsteps but there were none. And yet, something was there. Faras felt it too. Her ears pricked up in alertness and she trotted lightly. Here and there peculiar plants bore menacing looking flower heads. Jo was about to put his hand into one but its petals snapped shut suddenly like the jaws of a fish.

"I'm tired," Joe said as we walked through the dense undergrowth.

"Me too," said Kareem. "Let's stop up ahead in that opening for a while, it's getting dark."

"Agreed," I replied. "We could do with a fire, a bit of warmth. It's so cold and damp now the light is fading.

"I better switch Cube on for a bit. Cube, we need fire."

Cube opened its internal toolbox stored with useful gadgets and before us appeared the hologram of a nice small log fire.

"Wow," said Joe, "how did you do that? It feels real."

"As I go through the levels I come across useful objects and store them for later," replied Kareem, quite satisfied at the effect this was producing.

Just as we were enjoying our moment of rest a terrible smell drifted toward us. Cube said, "Dhegdheer located in the vicinity." Kareem jumped up, shut off the fire, and cried out, "Run," just as the creature, more terrifying than we could ever have imagined sprung through into the opening. She lunged towards us black as a shadow, her body several meters long, and lithe as a cat. Piercing yellow eyes and pointed ears protruded from a skeletal head and malnourished body.

Joe shouted out as she pounced, her talons reaching for him, teeth ready to bite. Faras reared up onto her hind legs between Joe and the Dhegdheer, giving us crucial seconds to flee into the trees. Grabbing Joe's hand, we ran urgently, branches scratching at our faces and arms. Joe was small and stumbled. The decaying forest was slimey under our feet hindering our escape. Faras galloped toward us, trying to gain pace but the demon was faster. I threw myself between it and Joe but she lunged toward me, coming at me through the branches. There was no escape. I believed I was done for and, holding up my arms in protection and squeezing my eyes shut, I said a silent, final prayer "*Bismillahir rahmanir Rahim* (blessings be to God)."

Just then, a noise shot beside my head so close to my face I could feel the air move. Then a thud. I opened my eyes in astonishment, one at a time, and there, dead on the floor, lay the Dhegdheer. Shocked, I turned around to see Joe lying on the ground with his catapult still aimed at the middle of the dead beast's head.

Irregular Friends and the Great Tree

Joe scrunched up his face as I planted a big kiss on his cheek. I'd never been so happy to see him with that catapult. Kareem shook his hand. "Couldn't have done it better myself," he said, deeply impressed with Joe's quick reaction. Pushing onward, we walked light-hearted, relieved from our escape but still a little shaken and growing increasingly more tired. We could see nothing but impenetrable trees and high up through the trees the far away distant sparkling of stars.

"What are we going to do?" I said finally. "There's no end to it, no way out!" I slumped to the ground taking off my shoes and massaging the blisters that had started to appear on my feet.

Kareem replied, "I thought you were a tough one, Aya. How come you are giving up so easily. We will find a way. Come on."

And as if he'd predicted it into existence, that's when we saw it. Up ahead in a clearing before us, stood a magnificent tree. Its roots sprawled into the jungle like gnarled fingers clutching the floor. It was so bulbous, aged and broad, it must have been over a century old. Overhead, its branches reached a canopy high into the heavens. Inside its gnarled trunk roots looked to be a small house. Inside the small house, an animal lay curled up amongst the roots.

"What is it?" whispered Joe, peeping into the shadows. "Is it another one of those things?"

"I don't think so," Kareem replied. The animal raised its sleepy head, stretching and yawning showing large incisor teeth, white as ivory.

"I think it's a cheetah," I whispered back. Just then two little squeaks could be heard and a pair of tiny cubs crawled out from beneath their mother and scampered curiously out to meet us.

Their mother stood and, stretching her athletic body, addressed us. "You are a long way from home," she spoke languidly.

"You can talk?" Joe said, surprised.

Anything seemed possible in this world.

"We are trying to find our way out of the jungle," Kareem said.

"Ahhh," said the cheetah. "I can tell you how to catch small creatures and hunt. I can watch the movement at night when the planets hide behind the clouds. This is my world. But I have become sick and must look after my cubs. Ask the serpent of the tree. You will find it in the next branch." And with that, she gently picked up her pups in her jaw, placing them back in the safety of the tree trunk.

"Can we help?" I asked but she was already huddled back in the tree trunk with her cubs, sleeping.

We looked above where a thick, dark branch twisted around the tree. "Come on," said Kareem, and grasping a root, climbed nimbly up in just a few movements.

"You make it look so easy," I said. Taking off my shoes I used my bare feet as leverage. Kareem held out a hand and a moment later we were sitting on a branch with insects flitting and buzzing around our heads. Joe clambered up after us.

"Where is it?" Joe asked. "The serpent?"

"Are you lllooking for me?" asked a lazy hissing voice.

Underneath us the branch twisted and writhed and we swayed, clutching to stay on. The snake was coiled completely around the branch and reared its giant cobra head.

"Oh, I'm so sorry," I gasped. "We sat on you."

"I have become trapped on this branch. Imagine that, me, clever and ssssupple as I am," said the snake.

We looked around and saw that a plastic bag had twisted into the coils of the snake's skin and ensnared it tightly onto one of the branches.

"How did this happen?" asked Joe. Taking a penknife from his pocket he began cutting at the bag, loosening it from the body of the snake. It slipped and slithered as he worked, trying to break free.

"Humans came through here long ago, and with them, came these things. There are many thousands of them littering the floor of the forest. That is when the forest began to die."

"Who came?" I asked.

"Humans in masks wearing white clothes. They came in their hundreddssss with large carts of poison. I know all about poisons. The venom of a snake protects it, wards off its enemies. This was not the same. Everything in the jungle has been dying. We are the enemy of no one and yet we will die soon. Many have done sssssso already."

"I don't know what's happening here," Joe said, "but we are going to do everything we can to help," said Joe. "Isn't that right?" He looked at us and we nodded agreement.

"Did anyone else come recently?" I asked?

"Yessssss. Just a ssssshort while before you arrived."

"Did the man have hair that stuck up and wore sandals?"

"Yessssss, I rather tthink he did," hissed the snake. "And whatsmore, he had a very yappy, noissssey dog with him."

"Did you happen to see which way they went?"

"Baboon knows about humans. He will hellllp you," Snake hissed and slid back down around the trunk in search of food and water.

"Did somebody call me?" A wise old voice boomed out across the trees and a huge Baboon jumped onto the branch and swung into the canopy above us. With white hair, a long, fiery red nose and two inquisitive eyes set close together, he was an imposing figure.

"Who are you?" the great animal asked.

"I'm Aya, this is Joe and Kareem. We are looking for our uncle and the Tomb of Qelhatat," I said, a little nervously.

"Call me Dameer. I have seen a human but I cannot help you. My family must have food. The fruit is rotting. This forest used to be plentiful but now we are beginning to starve. The trees which served us as homes and plants which provided for us have been dying for many years and soon we will lose the trees."

Joe searched through his backpack. "I have walnuts and cherries," He declared.

Dameer jumped down beside Jo inspecting the cherries and nuts, sniffing at them.

"You have more of these?" it enquired pawing at Joe's backpack.

"I have a whole bag of them. But you need to help us first."

Dameer narrowed his eyes and regarded Jo for a moment. "You killed the Dhegdheer? The whole jungle talks of it. Come with me," he gestured for Joe to jump onto his back.

"Wait, what about Faras?" I cried. "We can't leave her behind and it's too dangerous a journey for her alone. We are responsible for her now, we are responsible for each other."

"I will go with her," Kareem volunteered.

"We will protect you and the Unique Horn, have no fear for it. We are strong and nothing can approach without our knowledge," said Dameer. "But the safer route is through the tree tops. If the levels change you can become easily lost on the ground. There is not much time."

"Where are we heading?" Kareem asked.

"We will take you to the other side of the jungle. You and the Faras will leave soon. It is not safe to stay in one place at night on the jungle floor and your path is longer."

Dameer called out and within moments a group of baboons had come to escort Faras and Kareem. Faras shook her beautiful mane and bowed her head in ascent before they raced off through the trees together.

"Stay safe," I shouted out behind them, Kareem raised his hand and they were gone. We scrambled hurriedly upward on the back of the Baboons as they rose higher and higher through the canopy. For a long while we climbed past sloth bears sleeping languidly and squawking Toucans, parrots, and strange creatures I could not give a name to.

Above the wet mist we climbed after Dameer until the branches widened out and large hammock nests hung from the highest branches. Baboons sat with family groups, watching our arrival curiously, tentatively touching and inspecting us. They looked thin and sick.

"This way," Dameer guided us to a hammock branch of our own. Joe jumped off his back and we fell exhausted into the hammock. "I must meet with the elders to confirm a safe path for us."

Looking out over what was once a vast and magnificent Emerald Jungle, I could see that much of it was now dead black wood.

Sinister Corporations

Its office branch was located in Central London among the Georgian buildings that lined Whitehall looking out over the Thames. Big Ben and the London Eye could be seen by the gargoyles that looked down upon the streets, their dark stained faces expressions of terror and menace, melting from decades of acid rain. It was an organization that stretched back centuries and the board of Directors fathers and grandfathers had also worked for the company. Recently though, they had bought new premises in the tallest building in London and one that dominated all of Europe in size and reputation. On that day, they had held an emergency conference meeting to discuss the opening of the Gate by Uncle Benedict; an interference that had the potential to seriously hinder their plans and future profits.

A large screen opened up against the wall and all of the old fellows appeared like giants against it sitting around their huge polished wooden meeting table in expensive leather chairs. A younger man with dark gelled hair paced up and down in front of the screen, holding an espresso. His mobile phone was held in such a grip that it might have been attached to his hand.

On the surface of it, they were a reputable company helping the environment and making a substantial profit from the removal of industrial waste in England, their company logo was plastered across all of their letters, 'Rubbish is our Business.' But for decades, since the invention of the first Gate, they had broadened their reach into other worlds in order to find a solution for the increasing problem on Earth of toxic waste disposal. I can only guess, looking back, what might have taken place in those meetings, but it is certain that they would have been very concerned about the appearance of another Gate and what that might mean for the Corporation.

"Another Gate has been detected," Mister Vincent spoke to the wall of giants.

"What? How is that possible?" Moris replied, running his hands through his tufts of unruly blond hair.

"That snooping engineer, the one that worked for us in the past, must be behind it. Nobody else has the knowledge."

"I told you we should've finished him while we had the chance," Hunt replied leaning forward in his chair, his wig, which everyone pretended not to notice, had slipped forward.

Vincent spoke up, while surveying London from the windows of his high glass tower. "If he hadn't disappeared, we would have done exactly that! We searched for him everywhere. I've had my team on it for some time. He doesn't pay bills, use a bank card, own a house. He doesn't even have an email account that we are aware of."

"Well, fortunately for us," Hunt replied, "with your methods and technology not up to scratch," this was a dig at Vincent from his father and everyone pretended not to notice, "I've had someone working on it myself. Although he went off grid, we've been looking into some other avenues and we believe one has borne fruit, so to speak. We'll have him before long."

Vincent narrowed his eyes at his father. "A plant?"

"Exactly, never failed me before, you could do well to learn from your elders instead of relying on all this new-fangled technology."

"It was technology, Father, that secured the future of this company."

"It was physics boy, and science!" Hunt blustered, his already reddened face becoming more so.

Moris intervened in the little spat between father and son. "Did we ever find out how much he knew?"

"About what?" asked Hunt, lighting up a cigar and placing his feet on the table.

"About the woman?"

"My people shut that down quickly at the time. She was removed, limited exposure," replied Hunt.

"But the engineer was snooping around," said Moris.

"We cannot be too careful. Anything he may or may not have known was too much," Vincent spoke out.

"There are ways and means," Hunt crossed his fingers together into an arch and looked out over the Thames for an invisible solution, "and anyway a new Gate opening will only improve our position. If we can find it, we use it."

"You mean use both Gates?" asked Moris, helping himself to more trifle and sandwiches from the tea trolley.

"Yes, why not? We had a consignment agreed but now we can double it and double our profits." He frowned as Moris polished off the last of the trifle meant for two.

"But won't that poison the other world? We'd already agreed on toxic limitations. The Board won't agree."

Vincent replied, "The Board doesn't need to know. Anyway, do you think Huur cares about that? The trees and animals have been slowly dying for decades and probably soon the people and those Faerie creatures will become sick too if they haven't already. He doesn't care and it's his responsibility, his people, his planet. If he doesn't care, then why should we? It's no business of ours what he does."

"Well said, my boy!" Hunt congratulated his son for the first time. "The consignment will go sooner or later, why not make it sooner and we can all become richer much earlier than we thought possible. And you, my friend, can eat trifle to your heart's content," he pointed a finger at Moris.

"Let's get this toxic stuff off Earth and make it someone else's problem."

"But there is one thing you haven't considered," replied Moris.

"What is that?" Hunt and Vincent had his attention.

"What if HE finds the Gate first?"

Close to Losing Joe

As we rested, Dameer spoke to the elders of his tribe. I stood looking out over the terrible destruction of the jungle at the bleak tree stumps, like dying soldiers, protruded from a ground of black marsh. "I don't know what's happening," I said aloud, "but I need to find out. I'm starting to care about this place."

For a moment everything was still and quiet. I looked over to Joe as he started to fall asleep held by the hammock and I wondered if he was dreaming of home. Sectors B and A loomed above us. On Sector A, Volcano eruptions flared violently and I shuddered, wondering what kind of life might exist there, but on Sector B, the world of the oceans spun gently like the Earth. In the distance, where the desert dunes rose toward the horizon a metallic red and purple sunset spread hazily across the sky and land. Curled up next to Joe, and waiting for Dameer and the elders, I fell asleep.

When I awoke back home, it took a moment to realize where I was. It was lunchtime so we had only been gone a couple of hours of Earth time. I tiptoed downstairs to find Dad and Jennifer doing household chores. Sneaking out through the back door, I ran around the house, entering noisily through the front door and shouting goodbye to an invisible Uncle Benedict. "Hi Jennifer, Hi Dad," I kissed them both and poured a glass of milk.

"Did you have a nice time?" asked Dad

"Yeah great," I replied.

"Where's Jo?" asked Jennifer.

"He's gone upstairs. I'll take him some milk." Admittedly, this was all very strange behavior from me but I was too preoccupied to produce a better performance.

I rushed up the stairs to his room. Strangely, I realized I hadn't been to Joe's room before. The blue painted door was closed. I knocked and whispered, "Joe, it's me, wake up." There was no response. I knocked a little louder and when for the second time no reply came, I eased the door open, quietly tiptoeing in. The room was in darkness, curtains closed. It was quiet, too quiet. I crouched beside the bed to wake him but my heart sank. Joe was not there. It hadn't occurred to me that in taking Joe through the Gate, he may not be able to return. I was able to navigate in and out of the other world through sleep but the same was not true for Joe. "Stupid, stupid girl!" I admonished myself. I'd left him, I'd left Joe and I didn't know what to do. I looked around at the glow in the dark planets on his bedroom wall, at the model airplanes hanging from the ceiling, at the cuddly monkey hanging from the closet. I thought of how Joe's father had abandoned him and I started to cry.

Somebody was coming up the stairs. I wiped my tears on my sleeve and quickly left the room pulling closed the door. Seeing Dad on the landing I hurriedly explained, "Joe's really tired and he thinks he has a cold."

Dad was surprised. "Really, I'll just take a look, make sure he is not getting sick or something."

"No, it's fine, I took him some milk, he said please don't bother him, he just wants to sleep."

Dad frowned, "OK, if you think he's alright."

"He'll be fine," I said, hoping and praying that I was right. I needed to buy myself some time and get Joe back through that Gate. "Actually you know, I'm feeling quite tired myself already," I pretended to yawn stretching my arms out. "Probably the same cold that Joe has. I think I'll just rest in my room for a while."

Dad felt my forehead, "You do feel a bit hot. Jennifer and I were going to go to IKEA, we thought you and Joe might want to come."

"That is a great idea, Dad, you two go off and get some things for the house. I'll make Joe dinner and we can all have our own quality time, quality family time, away from each other. Kids need that you know sometimes…"

"Are you sure, if—"

I interrupted him, "Yes, we'll be fine, totally, happy, fine," I said as I led him toward the stairs. Dad went into the kitchen and I could hear them talking.

"I think Aya just needs time to get used to everything. It's all new for her. She's been without a mother for a long time," Jennifer said softly to Dad.

"Well, we have plenty of time to work it all out, together," he replied a little sadly.

But I was thinking, *time is the one thing we don't have,* as I waved Dad and Jennifer off in the car. Clouds were forming dark masses and a strong wind stirred. Turning back into the house I went to my room, closed the door, and leaned my back toward it.

"Let's get you back, Joe, safely before they realize you've gone."

On a Journey to the Edge of a Jungle

It was difficult to sleep worrying about finding Joe and returning him home. I reassured myself by remembering that so far, I'd returned to the same place at the same time so Joe shouldn't even notice my absence. But still I was worried about leaving him. Tossing and turning in my bed, throwing the blankets and pillows about me, I tried to get comfortable. I guessed that we only had a few hours before being discovered and didn't know how to find the Gate again on my return to the other world. Was it still open where we had come in? I doubted it since it had closed on us. The levels had already changed once, what if they'd changed again while I was away and where was the Gate now? Then I remembered what Uncle Benedict had said. 'Follow the signs.' I was going to need help.

My priorities were changing since the start of this adventure. Finding my mother would have to wait and so too the expedition to the mysterious Tomb of Qelhatat, whatever that was. Without Joe safe, well, I didn't even want to think what that. It was unimaginable. Not only did I actually feel responsible for him, but I was beginning to feel very protective too. *This is what it must be like having siblings. Concentrate, Aya, on the place you were last, the people you were with*, and at that, I drifted off into the other world.

When I woke up the sun was still going down and Joe lay safely beside me. Dameer was just returning through the leafy canopy.

"We can take you as far as the edge of the trees as agreed," he said. "The others are coming and will carry you. I'll take the boy."

"Is that where he went, Uncle Benedict? To the edge of the jungle?"

"Yes, it is the same path, though he took the harder route with the barking animal. The trees are dense and the marsh is now a poisonous quagmire. We believe he got through but cannot be certain. It is a dangerous and perilous route. If he made it, you will not be long behind him."

I thought of Faras and Kareem and shivered.

We clung to the backs of the Baboons as they leapt through the high treetops swinging swiftly from branch to branch across the vast jungle. The ground was a long way below us and I was scared but exhilarated trusting our friends to guide us. My arms ached but the view of the lands and planets made me forget my pains and I looked over to Joe to see that he knew the same sense of freedom.

It felt like hours before we reached the edge of the forest and my shoulders ached with the effort of holding on so tightly. Before us the trees began to thin out and red mountains rose out of the desert like canyons.

"Once there were great rivers here. We used to rely on this for fresh water long ago. Nothing lives now and it cannot give life," Dameer said sadly as we peered at the trickle of rust colored water.

Joe handed Dameer his backpack filled with nuts and fruits. "Thank you," he said. "We would be lost without you. We'd have never made it out."

"Your friends will arrive soon, they are not far behind." Dameer bowed his head majestically, took the food, and the Baboons turned back into the forest disappearing the way they had come. We waited for Kareem and Faras and when they finally appeared, we were all so relieved we laughed and hugged. I hadn't known if we were going to make it out of there but I kept those doubts to myself. And just at that moment, a haze came over the land and the landscape in front of us changed, taking with it the Jungle.

"Cube," said Kareem. "We need your help."

The Cube had never located someone off grid before and said it might not be possible. Since we didn't know quite which way to go, we sat down to wait for some reliable information. Besides, we didn't know what was lurking in this new level and it was better not to take any risks.

"Joe," I said. "I thought that was really kind of you and very clever too, what you did back there."

"The Dhegdheer?"

"Yes, and also the food. You've been quite useful, you know, for a boy."

"Thanks. You're pretty adventurous too, for a girl," he replied with a smile.

"I don't want to break up this wonderful moment between brother and sister but, there's something on the ground coming toward us." We stood next to Kareem who was looking far into the distant valleys and we saw it. A dark shadow advancing at great speed in our direction, blackening the ground like liquid oil. "I have a terrible feeling about this."

"What kind of feeling?" Jo asked uneasily.

"That it's coming for us." replied Kareem.

We looked at one another, nodded and I said, "run," as I grabbed Joe's hand.

To the left of us was open land, behind us the dying forest where I knew there was no escape and possibly even more danger. The only route was ahead, to the right and toward the mountains. As fast as we could, we ran. We reached the top of the hill and then I saw it, the outline in the rock. It was almost imperceptible. To anyone else it might have looked ordinary but I had seen it before. The drawing of the cave in Uncle Benedict's house and the caverns in the rocks leading into the mountains. It was a sign. We ran as fast as we could but the dark matter was gaining on us. We ran and tripped. "Run Joe, run to the rocks!" I shouted.

It approached us like a wave of fear. Just then, Faras appeared like a vision of beauty beside us. We leapt onto her back and she carried Joe and I toward the rocky outcrop.

"Kareem," I shouted behind us but I knew it was too late as he called back. "Go!"

"Nooooo," I cried out! The last thing I saw before the ground swallowed us up was Kareem being engulfed by the terrible dark matter.

Meet Me in the Cave of Shimbiraale (Cave of Birds)

"Stand perfectly still, don't say a word." A deep voice penetrated the darkness. The image of Kareem being consumed by that monstrous thing was more than I could bare. I could hardly see but Joe's hand was still in mine. Outside, we heard it, moving over the cave and, after some time, the sound of it faded into the distance.

"It's the birdsong from the cave, it confuses them. Come with me," the voice requested.

"But my friend…"

"You cannot help him."

"Is he…?" Joe asked.

"They have taken him," replied the voice.

"Where? Where have they taken him?" I asked anxiously.

"To the Dungeon on Sector A. That's where everyone is taken."

"But he is alright? They won't harm him?"

"For now. Who can say what those wretched things will do in the future."

"What are they?" Joe asked.

"The Jinn. They are agents of Huur, spirits driven by a thirst for distress made of dark fire and air. They can take on any shape, work alone or as a collective, feeding like bacteria on fear and hatred."

"We will have to rescue him, said Joe."

"Agreed. But first, Joe, I have to get you home. I don't know how, but I have to try. We need help. We need your help," I spoke into the darkness unable to see our rescuer. "Who are you?"

"My name is Biriir ina Barqo," he replied and sounded sad as if his name caused him pain to say it.

I felt around my neck. "Then I have something that belongs to you." Giant features appeared before in front of us and for a moment Joe and I stepped back in alarm. His movements were slow and careful, his dark huge eyes watched me.

"Do not be afraid," he boomed. "Show me."

I held out the necklace and a huge, rough hand with skin like tanned leather reached for it.

"Ahhh," he sighed, "my ring. He said it would be returned."

"Who said?" I asked.

He looked up again at me, away from the ring, sharp and quick and turned away into the darkness.

"Wait!" I said as we trotted after him into the depths of the mountain, led by Faras' light.

A pathway, carved inside the mountain, wound upward in a gentle slope through roughly carved tunnels, just big enough to allow Biriir's giant frame through. Hunched rounded shoulders, almost lost to the darkness, moved from side to side in great strides. As we ventured further, a sound, that was quiet at first, became louder like a small hum, the buzzing rose and it was impossible to know what could be responsible for it until we reached the opening. A low light appeared far in the distance and I strained to see what it might be. Shadows flickered over the stony walls as we approached a large cavern deep inside the mountain where the sound echoed off the walls. Small shafts of light dotted through the rock crevices from above. At first they looked like dancing lights illuminating the cave roof with silver blue. They flitted in and out of the minute shafts lining the cavern. Little silver baskets hung down making the whole place look alive, thousands of them flying to and from the nests. A city of birds.

Silhouetted against a fire on the ground was a man. Beside him a small dark shape appeared, turned at the sight of us and bolted toward us, panting, with its tongue out.

I jumped from Faras and ran flinging my arms around Buster, followed by Joe, and saw that the seated figure was my wonderful Uncle Benedict. After one big family hug we settled by the fire as Uncle Benedict began his tale relating what had happened since we last saw him.

"I awoke in the middle of the night. I can't say why, it was more of a feeling that something had changed. Throwing on my coat and sandals, I ventured out and saw a glow coming from the shed. I knew in an instant that what I'd been hoping for all these years was within my grasp. It was a great risk, of course. I couldn't possibly know if it would work or if I would be instantly incinerated. Throwing in a few objects that lay around, I tested that I wouldn't burn up as I walked through. It never occurred to me that Buster would follow. He had escaped from the house, as is his want, and as I walked through, it was too late to return him. We exited or rather entered into a cave. It was dark but there was a small boat. We rowed through and came towards the exit but Buster fell into the water and I jumped in to save him. We were pulled by a strong current out into a tropical jungle."

"The Emerald Jungle," Joe cried.

"I believe so, Joe. It was frightfully polluted and I was shocked and devastated. When I arrived, many years ago, Moonlight was thriving; a habitat full of life and wild animals, plentiful in fauna, invigorated and green. Imagine my dismay to see the terrible destruction inflicted upon what was once such beauty. There is very little jungle left here now and the planets are dying."

"But how has this happened?" asked Joe.

"Yes," I added, "you said you'd been to Moonlight before but you never explained when or why."

"It was about twelve years ago," he began. I was an adventurous and rather foolish and arrogant young man. I'd finished my PHD with acclaim and executives, important business tycoons who owned large companies known throughout the world, were lining up to offer me a position of employment. They praised my achievements and my work in engineering and creating inventions.

"One evening, late in winter, a man came to my home. He looked very important, in a suite. I saw his car parked outside was a Bentley and he had a driver. This man, gave me his card, said he had heard of my work and offered me a position before mysteriously vanishing into the mist. I'll never forget it, watching the mist swallow him up. Turns out his name was Hunt and he worked for a big corporation that were using toxic waste to make renewable energy. Well, I went to their offices in Central London, all very impressive, chandeliers, boardrooms, marble floors, historic famous paintings of important people in the field of Science. I'm ashamed to say, it impressed me and made me feel important and I took the job without looking into it."

As Uncle Benedict was talking, I was reminded of that night a few years before, when Mr Shah had visited Dad and I in London.

"So what happened? What went wrong?" I asked, eagerly.

"Within a few months I became suspicious of what the company were actually producing. They said they were working on new environmental initiatives. But for a, recycling company, they were dealing with a lot of chemically unsound materials. I was working on a project with other engineers, scientists and physicists. Neither of us knew exactly what the project was because we worked on our own part in isolation. The Corporation said it was for the exploration of other planets, some kind of space program but at the same time they were taking on more and more nuclear waste, more than was possible for a company to safely dispose of."

"They wanted to get rid of toxic waste in space?" Joe asked.

"That's what we thought at first, but then the disappearances started. Senior experts in our field began to go missing. They had one thing in common. They were all working on our project-renewable energy and waste disposal.

And so I began to ask questions, investigate. I couldn't do so openly of course but the more I discovered, casually asking questions of my colleagues, searching for clues, the more I unearthed. And then I found it, almost by chance."

"The Gate?" Joe asked, his eyes widening.

"Yes, Joe. One evening, I conceived a plan. I left my identity card behind at the institute on purpose so that I had a reason to return. There should have been no one around. The place should have been completely secluded but at the end of the corridor, I saw a mysterious light, coming from the lab. Naturally I investigated. I was very curious to see what was going on. The door creaked as I opened it, all good doors do in spy movies, and one of the engineers, a young woman was standing in front of an object, the Gate, as you call it. When she saw me, she realized her mistake and ran to close the door but I asked her to help me, let me know what was happening in the Corporation and told her of my concerns about what they were doing, and about my own work. I had been asked to engineer units that would hold and contain huge amounts of chemically unstable material but only for short periods of time. When I began asking what this material was, why it was being transported, and where would it end up, my enquiries were blocked. My concern convinced her to tell me what it was for, what she'd been working on because she was worried too. There was something so genuine about her. We discussed some of her equations, and her theories. She told me that she had been creating a formula for a device to transport people from one place to another."

"A teleport?" I asked.

"Of sorts." Uncle Benedict replied, "but more like a portal, a door."

"We met secretly and discussed how the project might succeed. And then one evening we finally did succeed in creating it. It was a frightening and wonderful moment. It was one of the greatest discoveries of our time, bigger than the discovery of black holes or extra-terrestrial civilizations. It was the biggest discovery known in human history!"

"And you had to keep it secret," I said understanding completely.

"Yes, we had to keep it a secret in order to protect one another and also to protect what might be happening to that new world."

"Moonlight," I said. Uncle Benedict nodded.

"What happened then?" Asked Joe.

"Shortly after that, she disappeared."

"Wow," said Joe. "Did you ever find out what happened to her?"

"All of her work was removed including the paperwork notes and equations that we had worked on together. When I enquired about her, the Corporation denied all knowledge of her whereabouts. Others were ready to believe their story but I knew differently."

"Did anyone look for her?"

"Of course, I went to the police but when they spoke to the Corporation, they said there was no evidence to suggest they had anything to do with her disappearance. We couldn't find out about one another then, I didn't know where she lived or who her family were because of secrecy. There was nothing I could do. I felt responsible, Aya, a responsibility to her for not stopping the Corporation. For not protecting her. I have to know what happened."

He did not look at me when he said my name. My heart was beating fast. I looked at Uncle Benedict straight in the eye and I asked a question that I already knew the answer to. "Who was the woman, the engineer?"

He returned my gaze. "Amel Ali. Aya, it was your mother."

Tears streamed down my face. I stood and turned away, walking down the tunnel.

"Aya!" cried Joe.

"Let her go, Joe, she'll come back."

"But will she be alright?" he asked.

"She's strong, like her mother," Uncle Benedict replied.

Buster ran after me and I let him be my companion. I walked the pathway that we had come by and found myself looking out of the cave entrance where the Emerald Jungle had once been. The fact that the Jinn were there only a short time before should have scared me but it didn't. I felt numb. Biriir came and sat next to me on the rock and said, "I know what it is like to experience the loss of a loved one."

Icarus

"It was long ago, before Huur and the System when the Ancients roamed the planet and people were free. He was not always a machine, Habbad ina Kamas, it is something he became, something he chose when Huur began his reign. He was a giant, like me, a friend. We were cousins and played together as children. Our families were happy ones, at least mine was. Our fathers were brothers. My father was ruler of two of the planets, now Sectors B and C. His father though, my uncle, was irresponsible, a drinker and brute who died at his own hand through gambling and brawling. He was strong and proud but liked to make trouble and was negligent in his duties. As Giants we had responsibility for our people, for their welfare, to protect. The great tribal leaders pledged to put their people before all other considerations and these traditions were passed down to them from their fathers. Fighting was how we proved ourselves and our strength. We would hold a contest yearly to show resilience, called the Great Iron Games, consisting of a triathlon of trials.

"That year my father, known as Bucur Bacayr, Habbad ina Kamas, and I were the favorite as contenders and would surpass all others by circumnavigating a volcano, felling and throwing the largest trees, and by swimming to a far out island and returning to claim our prestigious title. But there could be only one winner. We each had a strength that no other could surpass. My expertise, which I had trained for my whole life, was in walking the edge of a live volcano, risking plummeting into the terrible depths of molten lava. But I was fast on my feet then unlike today, I was not always the big clumsy oaf you see now, child. I was agile, young, fast, and had the best ability to balance and move quickly.

"My father won the contest for felling and throwing the trees. He found the largest in the whole forest, a great redwood, felled it in a second, such was his strength. He threw that weight half a mile. It was a great feat of the most incredible strength and he was well known for it amongst all across the lands.

"At that stage Habbad was placed third. He had fought commendably until then but he was a little younger and there was no hope that he would beat my father or myself at the final stage of the swim. I remember that day so clearly, as though it were yesterday. We were to swim to an island far out across the ocean. Rip tides lay between the mainland and the island and to fight against them was a test of pure resilience and endurance. Everyone gathered for the annual event and there was much excitement and celebrating. It was a matter of great pride to be chosen and there would be much feasting and merry making upon our return. But it was not without its dangers and we accepted this. The three of us entered the sea at the same time, a bugle sounded marking the beginning of the final race. We hit the icy water hard. It was a perfect day, a few waves but the sun bounced off the sea and it churned around our heads. We swam until the land could no longer be seen and the calls of the birds became less and less, we were so far from the land. What had started as a fine bright day began to turn dark. It was unusual for such a storm to appear so quickly but when it came, it did so with a great vengeance and force. We swam on. It was too late to turn back but also we had such pride, we could not be stopped and no one would admit defeat, we were so close to triumph. A Giants pride is his honor.

"Nearing the end we became fatigued and all were struggling to stay afloat but my father was ahead and just behind him Habbad hit a rip current and began to be pulled away out to sea. He was too proud to cry out for help and I was too far away behind to be of any use but my father looked back and could see that Habbad was in trouble and would most certainly have drowned. Without hesitation, he gave up his chance of winning in order to save Habbad. Using the last of his strength he swam against the current and rescued him. The two were just ahead of me, struggling against the waves crashing around them. My father's strength was great enough for both giants as they made their way toward the island. I was weakening but used the last of my strength to enter the island shallows. It was then that I saw something that has haunted my dreams and come to me in waking nightmares. As soon as Habbad knew he was in safe waters, he drowned my father, pushing his head under the water. It took a long time to kill him because he was so strong but my father fought.

"It was saving Habbad that had weakened him and given Habbad the advantage.

"My father's body was drawn under and taken out by the current. I stopped, paralyzed in disbelief in the sea a short distance from the shore and watched as Habbad stood on the island waiting for me. I knew that he would kill me too if he could. I had seen him after all. Did he plan it? Had he known what he would do or did his frustrations overtake him in a moment? It is impossible to say and in the end it didn't matter, the outcome was the same."

"What happened then, Biriir?" I asked, deeply saddened by his story.

"He claimed the title and told everyone that I had let my father drown. Perhaps that is why he swam back, leaving me behind him on the island or perhaps he was frightened that he would not win against me in a fight. Whatever the reason, his lie stuck and I was cast out of my own land, from my own people."

"But surely," I said, "they didn't believe it!"

"Some did, some did not. They were too scared. Sometimes power and strength are unstoppable. It suited some that my father and I could be removed and they could gain power for themselves and the status that comes with it."

"So what happened then?"

"I left. It was an unbearable shame."

"But that's not fair, Biriir, you'd done nothing wrong."

"Little one, my father had been killed, I was shamed. The truth meant nothing in people's eyes, only what was to be gained from it. I knew and I waited and if it took all of my life revenge would be mine. Giants know this. We have long lives we are not like humans, we can wait for centuries and we do not forget, nor do we forgive. And so I waited. I watched him become consumed by power. I watched him change from the youth I'd wrestled with to a tortured soul. It was that single act, I believe, that one decision made in the hope of gaining the trophy that changed him and set him on that path. It was to destroy him eventually. He became the machine you have seen, angry and full of hatred."

"And the ring, Biriir?"

"My father gave it to me that very day before the Great Iron Race."

"That is a very sad story, Biriir and I'm sorry for your loss. I'm sure that your father would be very proud of the person you've become." We sat in silence for a while. "What will you do now?"

"I will find him and I will kill him," Biriir said with utmost certainty.

"You lied to me," I said when I returned to Uncle Benedict. "You knew who I was all along. Our meeting couldn't have been a coincidence, could it?"

"Yes, I knew who you were, but not until a few days ago. How could I? Not until you told me about your dream world. I didn't know who your mother was. Jennifer and I never spoke of it and I'd never met your father. I have spent the last ten years, Aya, hiding, escaping that world, stopping it from finding me and then you walked into it and although it gave me great happiness, it also means danger for us all."

"Because the Corporation could find you?"

"I don't know, possibly. It seemed a very strange coincidence that your father met Jennifer and that you all moved out here."

I sat next to him and began thinking it through. I spoke aloud. "Who was it that introduced Jennifer and Dad? Who was it that got Dad a job at the place where Jennifer was working? Mr Shah! That slime ball Shah, this is all his doing! He must be involved with the Corporation in some way."

Joe said, "all that time, Dad and Jennifer thought that they were being helped, befriended, but it was all lies. It was arranged by someone in order to—what?"

"In order to find Uncle Benedict," I replied, "a man who had gone off grid, to escape, to not be found."

"Are we all in danger now then?" Joe asked.

We all looked at one another. I thought of Dad and Jennifer trying to wake Joe and finding him missing. I looked at Uncle Benedict. "Was my mother taken by Huur? I need to know."

"That is something I cannot answer, Aya, I'm sorry. I suspected that the Corporation were involved. If that's the case, they covered their tracks well and they lied. They kept the Gate secret. Who knows what else they've been covering up."

"Why would my father tell me she had died if she was missing?"

"To protect you, Aya," Uncle Benedict replied.

I knew that what he said was true. We all sat in silence for a while watching the flames of the fire become embers.

"I must stop the Corporation," Uncle Benedict spoke solemnly. "For over a decade I have been waiting for this opportunity to put things right, to save this place and this may be my one chance."

I nodded. I needed to make a decision. "I understand but you must know that I too have a journey. I cannot leave Kareem to whatever fate has befallen him and if my mother is here, I must find her. I have to find out what happened. But first, we need to get Joe back, he will be missed soon and we need to check that Dad and Jennifer are safe."

"That sounds like a sensible decision. Are we all agreed?" asked Uncle Benedict.

"I'm not agreed about the me going back bit," said Joe. We laughed and it brought some welcome smiles to a mood that had started to become very serious.

We sat thoughtfully together before the deep voice of Biriir punctuated the silence. "I also have some unfinished business and from what you have told me, I may also be of use. I will help you."

"So, the Gate only enters into this world in one place," said Uncle Benedict.

"But it closed when we came through," I reminded him.

I navigated the location for one single point in space so it should always open at that point.

"But the landscape is shifting, isn't it."

"Not exactly, it appears that the landscape shifts because of the game. It's like a sort of projection of a landscape over the top of the real one."

"So it should still be there, where we came in, if we can find it."

"Yes, the route back may not be the same but the gate should still be there."

"Well that sounds like a fun challenge," grinned Joe.

Not a Moment Too Soon

Biriir knew the country and the landscape better than anyone. It had, after all, belonged to his ancestors. He roamed it now with the walk of one who is resigned but not defeated. The System may have been imposed a game onto this land but he knew it as a person knows their own child and he was not easily wrong footed. He knew how the shadows fell upon the hills and was able to read the color of the sands. The levels of the game might move but underneath that the landscape remained the same. When the breezes blew, didn't they bring the scent of the earth? When the solar winds came, didn't they shimmer and radiate warmth as they always had? Each level was only one person's reality, after all. These were all things Biriir spoke of as we made our journey to find the Gate.

"So, essentially the System is like a big maze," said Joe, "but the entry and exit points stay the same."

"Yes, the levels appear and change differently for each person. Our job is to locate the Gate and navigate through the game levels to find it." Biriir said.

"What happens if a level has a big mountain sitting right on top of the Gate?" asked Joe.

"We will have to wait until that level changes in order to get to it," replied Biriir. "There is a shift in electrical currents," he informed us, "just before a new landscape is formed."

"Why do the levels move?" I asked Biriir, "why did The System not just keep the game in one place and have people move through it?"

"So that no one feels settled. They are moving all the time, going where they have been told. The System can control them more easily," Biriir replied.

What he said made sense. I was beginning to see the System as a giant maze being moved and controlled by something unseen, something sinister.

When we exited the cave, the landscape had already changed to dry savannah. Heading East, we walked for many miles with Joe riding Faras and Biriir striding far ahead of us. I was able to take stock of him better in the light of the day and was impressed by his wizened look. He reminded me of a red Indian Chief from the Wild West of America and must have been centuries old. His skin bore the character of the elephant and his great height towered over us all like an ancient tree. Giant leather boots gave him a hardy footing. He was not a person of the city but of the countryside, I thought, imagining him walking around Ely High Street and the excitement it would cause.

"What are we looking for?" I asked. We had reached a part of the plain with a single dwarf tree, striped of its leaves. There was very little else to go by but up ahead the ground rose slightly. Behind it we could see nothing. We followed his lead up ahead where the ground rose and fell toward low hills.

We were just reaching the top, climbing and puffing and panting. Biriir got there first. "Here", Biriir stopped. "The Gate is here," he said looking around us.

He stood silhouetted against the sky looking like a huge monument, but turned around to look at us and shook his head very slightly. "What is it?" Joe called out. "What's there?" We scrambled up the hill and reaching the top looked out over a vast ocean stretching as far as the eye could see. The sun sparkled over the water and we realized that our way out, our only way out of this place, for the safe return of Joe, was in the ocean.

Both Joe and I slumped onto the dry earth, our mouths agape. We were devastated.

"How long before another level shift?" I asked.

"Difficult to tell, hours days…and then we don't know how far away we will be from the Gate. It could crop up right next to us or the level will shift us further from it. Not to worry, not to worry," Uncle Benedict said, ever the optimist but looking at the sad and sorry sight of us all slumped in the sand staring at the ocean, I could tell he had no solution for this. Once more, one of the suns was beginning to set and it spread its strange half-light across the surface of the waves. As if to mock us, it was beautiful and all we could do was sink with it.

Suddenly, Biriir stood up and began wading into the water.

"Biriir, wait!" I called after him. We ran to the edge of the sea watching him wade deeper and deeper until the water splashed over his shoulders. Frightened that he would disappear beneath the waves, I called out. "Biriir, what are you doing?"

But he was older and wiser than I and took no notice. It was not too far from the shore and with his head still raised above the water he began searching the air before him holding his arms straight ahead as if feeling for something.

"It's here, close by, I can feel it. The air is different."

Suddenly before him, blue sparks erupted.

"I've found it," he declared triumphantly.

Neon lights flickered on and off showing the outline of The Gate and then disappeared.

"Quickly," said Uncle Benedict.

"Joe first," I said. Biriir picked up Joe and eased him onto his shoulder, returned to the Gate, and lifted him through. Like a magic trick, Joe disappeared as into thin air. Buster climbed onto Faras and she swam to the invisible spot. One by one we were ferried through and as we stepped back into Uncle Benedict's shed my mobile rang.

Ten missed calls. *Ugh oh, trouble! I hope everything's OK.* We'd been gone all afternoon. I answered, putting on my best performance. "Hi, Jennifer, are you and Dad OK? Of course, yes we are fine. At Uncle Benedict's yes, totally last minute plan. Yes, he's here." I handed the phone over to uncle Benedict with a grimace but nothing seemed out of the ordinary and they were more worried about us.

"Jennifer, sorry, yes, yes. Just turned up, last minute decision, you were at Ikea, should've left a note, yes sorry.

Joe, he's perfectly well." Joe stood there in a pool of sea water.

"I will be much more responsible next time. Of course indeed, right over. The police? Of course, understandable. Having too much fun. Didn't look at the time. Fishing, yes, of course, of course." He hung up the phone and we all looked intensely serious standing there dripping wet with sea water, a giant, a unicorn, a very damp dog and the rest of us, all soggy. Buster shook his wet coat over everyone and Faras had a big chunk of seaweed on her antenna. We all burst out in a roaring fit of laughter.

We'd made it back in the nick of time.

Gargantua

The Volcano sent molten lava and tumultuous flumes of boiling cloud into the dark sky. Inside the pyramid's fortress Huur stood watching from the balcony, his back faced the Jinn and wings flared out behind him like agitated flames. From here he could oversee the whole of his Kingdom and his army. No other building amongst the myriad of pyramids rose as tall.

They stood like white statues as far as the eye could see. An army, that would do anything he commanded without question. They were his creation and he was proud. Carved out of his terrible reign, the poor inhabitants had been poisoned for so long that they almost resembled ghosts. They were no longer human or animal but something in between, pliable and suggestable. It had not been intentional, a side effect of the radiation. The toxic waste had created this chemistry mingling with the air, minerals and metals on Sector A but how rapturous he became when he realized what was happening, how the inhabitants were losing their ability to think but gaining immense physical power. They were now his and he dreamed of taking them to conquer other worlds.

Steam from the pits of fire rose hazily over the ground, rising and falling with the beat of his wings like the breath from dragons. Behind him, the Jinn moved restlessly above the ground in-ever changing forms, blending and separating, human and animal, a mass of matter seething and writhing, serpentine.

"She is gone," an echoing chorus of voices hissed. "We detected her but she tricked us and found the Giant. She has gone to a place we cannot follow." They were enjoying the torment. Huur held no fear for them, and neither did any other living thing.

"She will come for you," they spoke as one.

"She is a child, she wields no power over me," Huur replied with just a little uncertainty.

"But she is of the Aayanie Tribe, one of the Ancients," the Jinn were delighting.

"And yet still, I have created this Kingdom, gained power over all living things." Huur's wings were raised in triumph against the world before him, against the Sectors beyond, rising for thousands of miles into space. His voice rang out, thundering.

For a moment there was silence.

And yet, they spoke in their gentle mocking, undermining tone, "You know who she can awaken. One more powerful than you." They swam back and forth in their swarm, a dark rippling changing body that sometimes shone and sometimes morphed into a black hole. It was difficult to tell how deep it went and how large it could spread, this unreadable mass.

Huur turned quickly and narrowed his eyes. "What do you say, boy?" he was addressing Kareem.

"Ah, well, hard to tell really." Kareem stood in semi-paralyzed fear. The last thing he could remember before waking up in the presence of the terrible and almighty Huur was seeing Aya, Joe, and Faras escape. He had willingly given up his freedom in order to see them to safety. "A fight between you and Aya? She's pretty mean when she's angry, but you are, well, a four meter giant falcon half person with magical powers so I wouldn't like to say who might come off worse. And I wouldn't call her a child, she might not like that."

Huur was not impressed. "Her weakness, what is it? Everyone has a weakness."

The Jinn wormed and spiraled their way around Kareem ,closing in around him, taking up the air, making it hard to breathe. "I see it in your eyes, hear it in your thoughts," they whispered. "A physical weakness, has she not? Breathing, her lungs, asthma."

"And what is your weakness, Kareem?" Huur came menacingly close towering over to peer into Kareem's eyes. Cube stayed silent.

To the Slipstream

Uncle Benedict convinced Dad and Jennifer to let us stay for a few days so that nobody would be concerned about us going missing and we could get on with our quest. It was not fool proof, but it was the best plan we had. We agreed to use the Gate again later that night. In the meantime we cooked up some food, bubble-and-squeak, from vegetables and potatoes, and fried them up with some butter. Biriir said he'd never tasted anything so good while Faras nibbled on hay, fruit and nuts in the garden. Drinking sweet milk tea on the porch, we had a quick conference to decide on our next plan of action.

"We all have different priorities, but our one aim is the same, to save Moonlight from Huur and the Corporation, correct?" I asked.

"Correct!" Everyone agreed.

"Biriir needs to find Habbad and I need to find the Tomb of Qelhatat, according to Fatima."

"We all need to get to Sector A though. That's where Kareem was taken and Uncle Benedict has to find Huur, who we think is there too," said Joe.

"True, Joe," Uncle Benedict replied, but the Gate won't take us there. There is no direct route that I know of.

"I can get you to Sector B," said Biriir. "There is a pathway known only to the Ancients."

"Then that's where we will begin," said Joe.

We all looked at him.

"You didn't think I was going to stay behind, did you?"

Despite our protests, Joe would not be left behind and we believed that, had we done so, he would slip through anyway and that would be a lot worse. So we decided to take him with us. Uncle Benedict lent Joe and I some clothes and we changed into t shirts with trousers tightened by a belt and woollen jumpers and boots that were too big but did the job.

Later that night, after we had rested, underneath an inky blue sky with stars twinkling like diamonds, we prepared to travel back, once more, through the Gate.

It was agreed that Biriir would go through first in case the Gate remained in the sea. He was a strong swimmer and resilient. He would check the lay of the land and come back through instantly to let everyone know if it was a safe.

We watched Biriir step into uncertainty, to return a few moments later giving a silent nod in ascent.

"Ready?" asked Uncle Benedict.

"Ready," we replied and once again I shivered a little as we stepped through into the unknown. We came out by the side of a lake that shone silvery blue and shimmered in the night air.

"The Slipstream is a rare phenomenon," Biriir explained, "it is like an invisible wave that flows between the Sectors, a force of gravity which will propel us towards Sector B." He drew a diagram for us in the sand, showing the great Sectors and their rotation. "Fortunately for us, the Gate entered close to the slipstream," and he pointed to a place on Sector C where we were now located. "We must watch for the planet alignment."

"How long will it take?" Asked Uncle Benedict.

"Days or perhaps hours," replied Biriir.

"Well, that fits in with our plans," said Uncle Benedict. "We will just have to wait now."

I looked up into the sky, to the stars and Sectors and thought of Kareem somewhere trapped and hopefully alive, he had to be alive, on the other side of another world. I thought of the night sky we had just left and I thought of Dad and Jennifer sleeping safely beneath it.

"But how do we get there?" Joe asked. "Will it just take us?"

"We need something," Biriir replied, "a device of transport to sail along the wave of the Slipstream."

And there on the shore behind us was a beautiful, shining boat, large and oval. "*Moonlight*," I gasped. This was definitely a sign. *Moonlight* had come through with us and it was not a coincidence.

"That should do the trick," said Uncle Benedict grinning. "How did you get here girl?" he said patting her fondly.

While we waited sitting on the shore, Biriir and Joe went to explore.

"Don't go too far," I said, "we will need to call you if the Slipstream comes." I was also fearful of the levels changing.

"What are we looking for?" I asked Uncle Benedict as we stared out across the ocean and into the nights stars.

"I've never seen it myself," he replied, "but I heard it's like a wave in the surface that produces a rippling effect like a mirage."

I looked over at him. "What are you going to do, Uncle, now that you got to return?"

"Put things right," he replied staring out over the ocean.

"But how, I mean it was so long ago?"

"Sometimes, time is your friend, Aya. All this time I was learning. Experience and understanding mean more than anything. If I'd come back all those years ago, I would have done things, made mistakes. I would probably have tried to kill Huur and that would've been wrong. It may also have ended my life or he would just have been replaced by another tyrant like Habbad. The only way to destroy the injustice is to return balance to the universe. The System has brought about a change that I helped to create. It should never have existed. People use to live together here in harmony, this place had a balance of its own where things flourished. We interfered with that for our own benefit, for power and greed. Those intentions will only ever result in destruction and unhappiness. Life is simple really, be kind, have good intentions, look after one another. The universe has a way of balancing itself. Huur was a good leader before he was overcome with arrogance and a desire for power. He couldn't get enough, he destroyed his enemies and then there was no one to question him. He became omnipotent, placed himself above everyone and everything."

"I think we may find what you are looking for, Uncle. If Fatima is right, the warriors on sector B, if we find them, may be able to help us redress the balance, InshaAllah (God willing)."

He smiled and said, "InshaAllah."

When it came, it was more of a movement in the air than anything that could be seen, like a ripple in the universe. We felt it. Uncle Benedict and I looked at one another and I jumped up and shouted out to Biriir and Joe. They had not strayed too far way and ran back urgently.

Biriir directed us and we sat heaped together on *Moonlight*. Suddenly there was a tug, a rush of air underneath us and Biriir launched us forward as though we were on a snow slope. The Coracle slid into the air and lurched upward. Biriir pushed away and it was just like being on a sleigh ride as we rose into the sky on invisible waves riding up and down, floating on the slipstream. We were off, speeding through the air toward Sector B, holding tightly onto our little boat chasing the waves that sailed toward high into the night. What awaited us, we were yet to discover.

Omnipresence

Voices of a million people filled Kareem's head with nightmares as he slept. They had entered his mind and mixed everything up, the Jinn. He could not say how long he had been like that and seemed to be carried along in a sweeping wave of distress and fear, falling in and out of consciousness. And then there was stillness. Pain stayed with him. It was a kind of distress he carried in his body so that when the voices and noise finally left him, physical weakness had taken hold.

"Level 500,000," Cube announced. "Hello, Kareem, I was beginning to worry about you. Your vital signs were fading and I had to stabilize you on more than one occasion. How are you feeling today?" Kareem pulled himself up, holding his head and leaning back against a padded wall. He was instantly sick.

"That's it, get it out," Cube said.

"Where are we? How long have I been here?" asked Kareem, once he had recovered himself.

"We've got ourselves in a bit of bother, I don't mind telling you," Cube replied. "You've managed to get us captured by the evil Jinn in order to save your friends and now we have endured a physical trauma that almost killed you, and myself. Though, strictly speaking, I can't actually die, just become dormant if my power is diminished for a long period of time."

Kareem groaned.

"We are now imprisoned for all eternity in a Dungeon in Sector A and will probably be killed by Huur once your friends arrive. At least, you will."

"Thank you for that optimistic update, Cube," replied Kareem. "I can tell that the whole experience has been very character building for you."

Kareem looked around the room. It was not the classical image of a dungeon he was used to in the game levels. It was not damp with chains and cobwebs and iron doors. Quite the opposite, in fact. This one was a white padded room with no windows and the slight outline of a doorway. "How long have I been here, Cube?"

"Two days, Kareem. Wait, there is something coming, a signal."

Kareem looked around toward the door.

"Not there…a message internally, coming through me. It is coming from inside The System."

"But that's impossible," Kareem replied. And indeed the Cube had to agree, it was impossible, and yet, it was happening.

"Incoming video message," said Cube as the screen in front of Kareem's viewer flickered. A woman's face appeared, the similarity of her look and features with those of Aya was striking but she was older and Kareem knew instantly who this must be, there was no question. She was very beautiful but strain showed around her eyes and she was very pale.

"Kareem, I must be quick, there is a danger that we will be discovered. I am not the only person working as an engineer on the System," Amel said.

"Have you been manipulating the levels?" Kareem asked.

"Yes, I needed you here and Aya, but I also needed to keep you both safe. I have called you, changed routes and landscapes in order to lead you to Sector A."

"Why? What have you brought us here to do?"

"You have met her, Aya, you know that she is special."

"She is determined and courageous yes, that is why I agreed to help."

"But there is more, she is more than that."

"What do you mean?" Kareem asked

"She is born of The Ancients, an Ayaanie."

"But they are a myth!"

"No, they belong to the Sectors, a time before The System existed, an ancient tribe."

"The Aayanie, the angels?"

"Yes."

"What do you want from me?" Kareem asked.

"She is the key, the only one who can awaken Nidar, the only one who can save us."

"Save us from what?"

"Huur is going to destroy the planets and try to escape to Earth. What he intends to do there is anyone's guess but it cannot be good. He will take his army. Everything and everyone will be destroyed."

"But how are you involved?" Kareem asked.

"Huur found me. He knew I could be of use to him not just in order to create a new world but also to destroy the old one."

"You helped him to poison the planets?"

"No, I helped him to eradicate the old world by removing all evidence of it, by destroying all written records of it and by creating The System."

Kareem sat back. This was too much to take in all in one go.

"I had to search for all evidence in files, stories, myths, registers of life, death, marriage and destroy them, replacing all records with the new rules of The System"

"Are you saying that nothing outside The System exists?"

"There are still remnants of the Ancients that have been in hiding. I have been protecting them but if Huur is allowed to continue, he will not be held back. He has destroyed their history, their present, and soon, he will destroy their future. He will destroy everyone."

"Why now, why did you not stop him long ago?"

"I could not, Huur has great power. Nidar is the only one powerful enough to hold Huur back, he has become like a God creating a world where only his will exists."

"And Aya?"

"Why do you think I am here, helping Huur. I would not do so willingly. Huur has ways of forcing people to his work."

"He threatened her?"

"He would take her life and my husband's."

"Does Huur know about Aya, her power?"

"Yes, but he sees her as a child and underestimates her. In truth, she is the only person remaining that can awaken Nidar but it is a very small hope that she can do so. She is still a child and may be too young. I have not called her before for this reason and in order to protect my child. But there was no other hope. Huur is preparing something and if we don't act now, it will be the end."

"What if she fails?"

"Certain death for every living thing on the Sectors and possible destruction of the Earth"

Days of the Ancients

"It used to be, long ago," Amel said to Kareem, "that each tribe, in the world of the Ancients, had a special power.

"There were the Giants, who had incredible physical strength and lived on what we now know as Sector C, alongside the jungle animals and the great forests. They built magnificent cities and banqueting halls, held ceremonies and games to show their might and monumental strength.

"On Sector B in Subterranean, the warrior Faeries could foretell of any impending disaster and speak to the clouds and the oceans and all species of nature including flowers and plants. They were, and still are, formidable warriors, although there numbers now are also greatly depleted. Those who have seen them describe a creature, half human, half butterfly. I have heard that their bodies sparkle silver and gold and all the colors of the rainbow and that, despite their great beauty, and delicate appearance, they are the fiercest of warriors."

"More fierce than the Giants?" asked Kareem.

"In some ways, yes, because they are so agile, fast, and quick-tempered," replied Amel.

"What about the Jinn?"

"Well, as we know the Jinn are pretty cruel and thrive on distress and fear. There is not much that can harm them but it was not always that way.

"On Sector A lived the Ayaanie. They spoke a secret language that no one else could decipher except the ruling Spirits who also lived there. They were so ancient that everyone went to them for knowledge because they were older than the stars and had great wisdom and power and advised the people. The Ayaanie were the interpreters between the people and the Spirits and passed down their abilities through their children. Their ability did not come in words but was intuitive and they connected silently, telepathically. And so the Spirits could only communicate with and through them, and the Ayaanie had a place in the world communicating their messages and advising the tribes on matters regarding their daily lives. But, as with any civilization, there is good and there is bad and the bad Spirits grew restless and jealous of the harmony created between the Ayaanie and their own people who had good intentions and some of them wanted to disrupt it, corrupt, and cause chaos.

"And so, they whispered bad things into the ears of those who would listen and steadily manipulated and disrupted communication between them.

"In doing so, they rose to power and began using those such as Huur and Habbad who were already paranoid and full of fear and hatred and rage.

"As the years passed, Huur began his destruction of the Sectors and wiped out many people until there was no way to talk to the good Spirits and ask their advice and so the people and animals became less, and the great Spirits slept more until one day there were too few Ayaanie and no one came to speak with them. The Tribe still exists but there are very few. They have spread over many worlds and scattered and the intuitive language is dying. When I first came to this world, I took Aya back with me. She was alone and had been abandoned. She is older than she looks because Ancients take a long time to age."

"Does Aya know any of this?" Kareem asked.

"No," Amel replied. "And she must not find out. Not yet."

"Why are you telling me this?" Kareem asked.

"Because I need your help."

Entering Sector B
The Sa'ad ad Din Islands

The giant Cube of the planet on Sector B was alerted to our entry as we flew within its atmosphere. From a distance it had looked solid but as we moved closer we could see that its barrier was much more like an electrical force-field. Beneath us, a carpet of ocean blue covered the planet peppered with lush green islands.

"They are the Sa'ad ad Din Islands," said Biriir. "They stretch across the planet. Each one is a homestead for the Faerie Warriors."

"How will we ever find the Tomb of Qelhatat?" Joe asked.

"It is a long time since I came here," replied Biriir, "but I am not without knowledge or friends. We will find what we are looking for, or they will find us."

It was a reassuring answer but still, there were thousands of islands and at this distance, they all looked very much the same and we didn't have much time. We had to find Kareem fast before something bad happened, if it hadn't already.

We sped through the sky, through the layers of clouds, which I touched, my hands passing through the invisible candy floss. The air smelt like the sea, salt, and holidays as we hurtled toward a beach on a small island, arriving with a great bump and bouncing a few times before being tipped out onto the sand and coming to a complete stop.

Buster and Faras shook themselves off and Faras sneezed sand from her nose. Finding my feet and brushing off the sand from my clothes, I took in our surroundings. The island was breathtaking, like a garden of paradise. Palm trees blew softly in a gentle breeze under a warm sun and pure blue azure sky.

The aqua lagoon shone like crystals. For a moment, everything was still and beautiful with only the music of waves washing softly against the shore. It did not last.

Suddenly, another sound penetrated our paradise, shattering our peace. We glanced around. There was no time to lose. From below the sea, an alarm had sounded all around the island and as we turned, something emerged, rising menacingly up through the surface of the water. It was the Jinn. We were totally surrounded. As if that wasn't bad enough, a familiar thundering screeching sound alerted me to someone I had not seen for what seemed like a lifetime. He rose steadily from the water behind the Jinn and was advancing toward us at great speed. It was Habbad ina Kamas, Biriir's lifelong enemy.

Biriir straightened himself up to his full height. It was too late for escape. There was nowhere to go. Habbad and the Jinn were almost upon us in seconds. Buster crouched low, barking and growling. The Jinn stretched themselves out into a terrifying dark line blotting out our view of the horizon and forming a wall as they moved toward us, a wall that would be impenetrable. Our exits blocked, all we could do was move backward into the middle of the island, forming a small circle for protection.

"What now?" I cried.

"Difficult to say," replied Uncle Benedict, "we appear to be in a bit of a tight situation. Any ideas, Biriir?" he shouted out behind him, but Biriir had a situation of his own to deal with and it was pretty immediate. Habbad was coming straight at him in full battle mode, raising his weapon and firing it, just missing him as Biriir threw himself sideways. The ground shook at the impact sending sand and water flying into the air. He leapt up with an incredible agility and the two giants crashed on impact as Biriir and Habbad collided, full on rolling and thrashing with the sound of metal screeching. Across the beach they thundered, wrestling, throwing punches, and roaring with rage like lions. They were formidable. It was terrifying to see these two great giants in battle.

Meanwhile, the Jinn had us surrounded and as they closed in on us their chorus of screams grew louder and more terrifying. I held the coracle close, hoping for a moment when we might still break free and catch the slipstream but I was frightened for Biriir, at leaving him. I couldn't believe that Habbad could get the better of him but I could not be certain. We watched paralyzed as the height of the Jinn grew, rising like a tsunami threating to engulf us to such a degree that I felt it unlikely we would be able to break through.

"Move back," shouted Uncle Benedict as the Jinn closed in blocking out the light. We did so until we were entirely surrounded, encased, and it looked like, this time we were truly done for.

"What are we going to do?" Joe cried out over the terrifying sound of the Jinn. We held our hands over our ears and sank back against a group of palm trees in the middle of the island, now our only protection, just as the Jinn blocked out the last of the light around us. It was like being in a tunnel of darkness.

"Biriir," Joe shouted.

He ran to us with Habbad clinging to him, dragging him backward. He broke free and forced his way through the Jinn engulfing us but they were too powerful and blocked his approach.

"Fatima, where are you?" I shouted out into the darkness, "I need your warriors now."

Suddenly, the Jinn stopped just when the last point of light above us was diminishing. A hole broke through them and a scream erupted, one voice piercing the wall. Like melting plastic the hole began to peel back and let in the light and through it, the oceans parted around us. We were astonished. Riding at the head of the waves, a site too beautiful to be true. Dozens of Faerie warriors dressed in battle gear hovered before us, their strong wings shining golden under the sunlight. A magnificent army, led by a Warrior Faerie, were hurling cubes of electric blue fire at the Jinn.

"Wow!" said Joe.

The rest of us stood there in awe, mesmerized by this heavenly sight and, just for a few seconds, forgot our perilous situation.

They had the Jinn surrounded. Rage and confusion rippled through them to see this army that dared to attack, that dared to intervene. The circle surrounding us was collapsing. On one side of it was the enemy sent to kill or take us. On the other side, what we hoped were our friends and allies. They did not wait for an invitation and launched headlong into full battle. The Jinn flew at their attackers spreading their darkness out like a cloak trying to encircled and enclose the Faeries but the warriors already had them surrounded and blasted more holes into them with their blue flames of energy.

I would like to say that we helped, that we made a difference, but this battle was one we could have little impact upon. We had no weapons and were small and weak between these great powerful beings.

Biriir and Habbad fought on. They seemed equally matched in strength though Habbad had his casing and laser, Biriir had the strength and determination of many years of harbored rage. He had gone through this battle in his mind, over and over and like a chess match, had anticipated Habbad's moves. Biriir was not fighting move by move, he already knew and was prepared for the last and final checkmate and every blow that Habbad dealt and believed to be a small victory, Biriir was allowing him in order to get him where he wanted. Into the ocean.

Joe and I clung onto Faras, galloping and leaping out of the way as the two Giants hurled themselves at one another across the tiny island, the earth crashing and thundering around us with the impact. The Faerie army stood, incredibly fierce and foreboding before the Jinn who were rising up again before us, preparing another attack.

The two giants rolled into the water and Biriir hurled Habbad out into the sea where Habbad could not use his laser and was hindered by his armor. Before Habbad could recover himself Biriir gave an almighty roar, throwing himself onto Habbad and using all of his weight to push him under the surface of the water. The two giants disappeared beneath the ocean surface, whose waters boiled and frothed, and we could only guess at the turmoil underneath. They rose up but fell under the surface of the sea once more.

"Biriir," I screamed as the waters suddenly stilled. Several minutes passed by and I watched in horror. I tried to run into the water but there were Jinn everywhere and I could not reach him. I believed that Biriir had given his life to remove Habbad of his.

Just as I had given up all hope, exploding to the surface with a great gasp Biriir came up, alone. Our eyes met, and I knew that what he had sought to do for so long, he had done and now he was depleted. There was no victory in his face, only pain.

But our own battle was not over. The Faerie Warriors had surprised the Jinn with a new power source, previously unused and they were not ready for it. The Jinn had to reform into shapes, but this took energy and time and they were having to adapt quickly. Their confusion slowed them down.

Surrounding us and forming a protective circle, the warrior fighters led us toward the Coracle, while continuously firing and pushing back the Jinn. Their leader hovered before us protectively. She was beautiful and majestic with wings the color of a Kingfisher, sometimes flashing golden and sometimes green.

"Quickly, we have no time to lose, we can only hold them for a short time. We must get you to safety," she spoke with urgency and we were fast to act. We leapt onto the Coracle turning it toward the slipstream, collected Biriir, and sped away into the air. With a lurch we flew rapidly upward and as we were just high enough, passed over the island flying out over and across the ocean.

We could see the battle still raging on; was it my imagination that somewhere at the bottom of the ocean, the outline of a giant, lying in his watery grave?

We flew on before hurtling, once more, toward the sea and making an undignified landing with a huge splash into the water.

"There has to be a better way to travel," said Joe, spluttering, drenched in water from head to toe.

Fins appeared in the water, circling the coracle. Suddenly a dolphin launched itself into the air and performed a twist and dive, only to disappear again into the sea. Then more arrived, one, two, three, four more, ducking and diving through the waves. A conversation seemed to be taking place between the dolphins and the Faerie Leader.

"Hold onto our sea friends," she instructed.

We clung onto their fins as they sped off further away from the island, away from the battle and towards safety.

Subterranean

The tropical island was larger than the one we had initially landed upon. We sat on the shore and thanked the dolphins for an exciting sea journey. I thought how, if times had been different, I could be on holiday here in a beautiful paradise. Some of my friends at school had spoken of going to places like this, Thailand, Maldives and I thought of them now so far away. At least that's how it felt. In truth I was just a breath of Moonlight away from Earth.

"There is no time to lose. We have escaped the Jinn for now but they are powerful and will not be held back for long," said the Warrior Faerie. "You must follow me, I know somewhere where you will be safe, for a while at least, and there is someone whom you must speak with." I wanted to ask her about Fatima and my mother but she moved so quickly ahead, I could barely keep up.

We reached the top of the beach, our wet clothes drying quickly under the heat of the sun. Faras and Buster were covered in salty sand, as we entered the jungle of banana, coconut, and date palms. Winding through small streams under the shade of the leaves, we made our way toward a lagoon that led to a cooling waterfall.

"Wait here," she ordered as she dove into the crystal blue waters disappearing for a moment, before reappearing. "It is safe, they will allow us passage," she replied. "Come."

"Errrr? I'm not jumping in there," Joe said. "There could be anything in there, piranhas, sharks, crocodiles, anything!"

"Trust me," the Faerie said smiling, "I will allow no harm to come to you. You are very precious to us. Nobody comes to the island unnoticed, we are forever on our guard. If you were not with me the sharks would have 'prevented' you from entering. They can be very persuasive."

"I think we should do as she says," Uncle Benedict said, "anyway, we don't have a great deal of choice in the matter, there is nowhere else to go."

Holding hands in a chain, we jumped into the lagoon together, sinking into the cool soft water with Buster and Faras jumping in too. For a few moments, we held our breath and sank under the fresh water. Swimming forward, we resurfaced in a whole new world, into a secret cave.

Large bubbles surrounded us, pockets of air underwater. Sparkling jewels shone from deep blue greens and purple shades. It was like a city of treasures, like candy floss and quality street chocolates. Rocks and walls glistened moist with the colors of the sea. Valleys of sea urchin and emerald and ruby seaweed pathed the underwater landscape. A valley flowed as far as the eye could see that seemed to stretch far, far beyond the reach of the land we'd seen from above. Fish swam around us as if by magic. Giant Stingray, with white bellies and black backs covered in stars, passed over our heads, their tails trailing long behind them. We seemed to float on air as we walked out into this astonishing world that defied the laws of nature.

"Are we underwater?" Joe asked

The Warrior Faerie smiled. "Those rules don't really apply here. Some of them are the same as the natural laws on your Earth but there are also a few surprises."

Even Faras was a little confused. She was trotting but her hooves did not touch the ground. It was a kind of air swimming. Buster and Faras' bubbles kept bumping into one another and Buster began acrobatics. We copied and started running, jumping, and trampolining and Joe and I giggled like I never remember having done so before. Not since Mum was around. *Mum*, I thought and began to feel serious again.

"I wish Kareem was here," said Joe. "I wonder if he knows about this."

"We will have to find him, won't we, and we can bring him here," I replied.

Faras did a back flip and floated upward and we had to catch her tail and pull her back down again.

Moving gracefully through the sea we followed the Warrior Faerie toward, what looked like a palace in the center of all the aquatic life, made from the wrecks of old sunken galleons. Yellow and black striped fish and clownfish swam passed us and turtles flew gracefully overhead.

"Is that where we are heading?" asked Uncle Benedict, pointing to the palace.

"Yes, the Tomb of Qelhatat. We could not come any other way," explained the Warrior Faerie, "it must be kept secret and protected."

"I never imagined it would be under the ocean," I replied, "and it is unpolluted."

"It has not always been so. Huur tried to use Sector B in the same way that he has poisoned Sector C but we fought him, held him back. At first it looked as though the planet would die. Our seas became polluted with poisons and plastic waste brought through from the other world, your Earth. We could not understand why a people and their tribes would create such substances that could destroy worlds and kill creatures but we understand that they would want to rid their own world of them in order to retain nature and balance. We could not reconcile our world to live and exist with these things and so we decided to use the negative and dangerous atoms that lie within them, neutralize them, and create a purer energy that could be of use to us."

"A renewable energy! And that is what you used against the Jinn?" Uncle Benedict asked, impressed.

"It is in its infancy, but yes. We have created only small amounts of it."

"How does it work?" Uncle Benedict asked. "And why has it not been used in Sector C?"

"As a neutralizer it does not destroy negative atoms, it prevents them from energizing. The energy still exists but it can have no effect and that's why you saw spaces appear within the Jinn. The energy no longer had force to exist in its full capacity or draw on its power. You ask about Sector C?

Unfortunately too much damage has occurred and the nuclear poisons are beyond our ability to correct. We are unable to neutralize such destructive elements. Only the ancient Jinn have that power and so we can use small amounts of recycled energy but are limited in the use of it. We are few and our abilities lie in our ability to communicate with nature, we have no great powers to restore."

Moving forward with the tide, the bubbles drew us into the hull of a huge sunken ship covered in ancient corals, star fish, and sea urchins like the blooming flowers of an ancient sea garden. Giant octopi guarded its entrance, their bodies shimmering in changing colors camouflaged and vibrant. Their tentacles holding spears and reaching out to stop us before agreeing to let us through.

"Who is the Queen of Qelhatat?" I asked.

"There was a time when Faeries were seen as less important than other tribes, of lower status. Children were separated from their parents at birth and brought up, trained to become servants. Queen Qelhatat had been treated harshly by her masters but was born with a spirit that could not be subdued and she began, as a child to fight back. By the time she was your age she had led an army into battle against their oppressors."

"Wow," said Joe, "she sounds fierce."

"Who were the oppressors?" I asked.

"The Jinn of course," she replied.

"Why did Fatima send me here, seeking her?" I asked.

"Ah yes, you spoke of Fatima and that is why we rose to help you. She is a sister of ours, sent to Sector C long ago to assess the damage of Huurs poisoning but also to wait for your arrival. She has been looking for the ancient ruins outside of The System and logging the information that was lost to us, destroyed by Huur."

The Warrior Faerie turned to me. "We need your help, Aya, Huur cannot be reached directly, doing so would mean certain death for us and for you but there are ways known only by warriors, ways passed down through generations, Queen

Qelhatat will explain more to you, she has more knowledge than I."

As we were swept inside the galleon, curious creatures swam close to our bubbles to gaze at us. Through the dark and broken wreck we drifted until we entered a large open space that would once have been a large galley. Electric jellyfish lit the cavern and there, amongst corals and seaweed, was the Faerie Queen Qelhatat. It was not to be doubted. She was ethereal, translucent like a fish, but her wings were so glorious, golden, and powerful that she glowed and shimmered in the water like a jewel. Golden hair floated around her body like a mane. She was most definitely a Queen.

The Tomb of Qelhatat

She looked at me directly with a gaze that seemed to search deep into my soul and I shuddered.

"I will speak with the Ayaanie alone," she instructed. Uncle Benedict and I looked at one another and Biriir said, "We will not leave her. We stay together or you will speak with no one."

"What I have to say is only for the girl," Queen Qelhatat said.

I smiled at how protective Biriir had become of me in such a short time. "It's OK, Biriir, Uncle, Joe, let me speak with her. You have a look around and we can catch up in a little while."

Reluctantly, they left and the Queen and I were alone.

"Moonlight calls only the chosen few. Do you know why that is?" The Queen sounded wise.

I didn't know, and I said so.

"Everyone that is called here, into this world, comes because they are seeking something."

"What about those who are not called?" I asked.

"Then perhaps they are not destined to be here," she replied with a serious expression. "So, you come here seeking your mother," she smiled knowingly. "Sometimes we think we know what we seek but we do not. I could tell you of life and loss of the warrior princess but then you know of what I say and have lived more than sadness in your days, little one, warrior child keeping her memory alive. She seeks you too though not as you may imagine."

"What do you mean? Where is she?" I asked.

"I would tell you in the hope that you will awaken Nidar from the underworld on Sector A." She held out some images made of a peculiar material like a soft carved wood but thin and very flat. Lines and geometric shapes were etched into their surface. They made no sense to me and I could not understand what they might be or how they might be used.

"Is this a game?" I asked. "Some kind of map or puzzle? You have handed me these with a cryptic message but not answered my questions." I was becoming frustrated. Each time I thought I was getting closer to finding my mother, something new arose. "I just want to find her, be with her, but everything is in my way."

"Child, she never left. You are filled with sorrow but what you do not see is that there are many ways in being with someone, to hold heart and treasury. She did not leave you, my dear, you left her."

"But she died, at least I thought she did. I don't know anymore."

"She gave you everything you needed to keep her in your heart and mind but in your pain you only felt the flames. She is you and you are her while you exist then so does this. Did you know that jellyfish float to the shore and their dying cells produce living spore? Our cells are from stars, from meteors. More exists than our ego. More than our small needs. All of this feeds the universe."

"I just want my mother!" I sobbed.

"And you shall see her again but in doing so there will be pain and in sacrifice comes gain. The cost is never free, warrior child."

I thought a moment about what she implied before asking, "And what is your purpose in being here?" She looked at me with narrowed, intelligent eyes.

"A good question for one so young." Her strong wings fluttered up and down before she replied, "I was born into this world to help others and gave my life to the tribe. They will worship me and I will lead them but will never gain freedom. I am a Queen. You, however, can free us all should you awaken the Nidar. What you do after that, well that is to be seen."

"Who is Nidar?"

"One of the Ancients, a powerful spirit, more powerful than Huur and the Jinn," she replied.

"Why me? Why can't you just awaken this Nidar yourself if you are a Queen? I am just a girl. What you ask is too great a challenge for me," I was becoming increasingly tired.

"Ah, but are you though? Do you not know from where you came, the Ancient Tribe who've lost their name?"

"Fatima told me that my name comes from an ancient tribe," I replied.

"Yes, and you are unaware of the powers that you possess. Inside lies an ancient language of signs and symbols, a tongue that can speak with the Spirits. You are one of the only ones left, child, that can do this."

I thought about my dreams since childhood. I thought about the signs that had helped to lead me here.

"You must use the pieces to find the Legendary View. It exists on Sector A and will be the key to summoning Nidar. You must find it. But, if you are a second too late, it will be gone and Nidar will remain dormant."

"But how is that even possible," I almost cried. "You have handed me something I don't understand and I cannot do it, I cannot."

Queen Qelhatat looked at me with her head held slightly back. "Then you are not the one to summon Nidar. You are not of the Aayanie, for the Aayanie are brave and fearless."

"Perhaps, I never was!" I angrily turned to leave which is very hard when you are in a bubble under the ocean. This was ridiculous, it was unfair. "I am only 13 years old, why is this being placed upon me? I want to go back home, go to sleep, and wake up thinking of Ely and the Fens, playing on the boat, throw sticks to Buster, eat tea and cakes in the theatre!" And at this memory, I sobbed out loud thinking in shame of how I had hated it, how I wanted it to all go away, and now this was all I longed for, that and my mother and Kareem to be safe and free.

I turned around. "I can't do it," I said, "give the job to somebody else. I am not the person you are looking for." She watched me as she fluttered pacing from left to right, keeping her eyes on me.

"Some of us doubted you. They said, how could one so young do so much. She is just a minor. One of those that believed was a young minor also. One who had been taken from Earth as a youngling, one drawn to help you at the bequest of the warriors, one who would make his own sacrifices."

I frowned. "What? Who do you mean? Kareem, do you mean Kareem? Kareem is from Earth? Has he been helping me because of you?"

"He believed in you, your honesty, your courage all along but I suppose he will die in that belief, in a Dungeon in Sector A. When you leave, Huur with have no further need of him as bait for information. Death will be instant or he may be left in the dungeon for a century, kept alive in torture, alone. If Moonlight survives that long."

"Stop it!" I screamed. "Stop it! That's not fair, you can't blame that on me, what Huur does is not my doing."

"Listen to me, child, you have been raised an Earthling, and therefore we can forgive you. But one thing I will not tolerate is cowardice."

"But I can't do what you ask!" I said helplessly.

"You gave up before you started, that is not the sign of a true warrior. That is not the trait of a messenger, an Ayaanie that speaks with humans spirits and Jinn." And with that she turned and left.

I stood there alone in a bubble under an ocean in a foreign place and a small voice grew inside me. 'She's right,' it said, 'what do you have to lose? Maybe you aren't the one, maybe you can't do it but if you don't even try then Kareem loses his life, your mother will never know you.' I looked at the space that the Queen had left. I paced up and down in my bubble cursing myself and I shouted into the air that she had left hoping that I wouldn't regret this for the rest of my life but also knowing there was no other way. "How do I get there?" I said finally. She had obviously been waiting, because she appeared immediately.

"Now that is the question of a warrior." She smiled knowingly.

"Nidar is the one to speak and guide you as you seek. To awake the Jinn is itself a danger for whoever looks for unknown danger but you must be or destroyed you will most certainly be. Huur is no simple foe as everyone in the sector knows.

"The others can accompany but only you alone may gain entry to the place where the Jinn and the Aayanie meet, where heavens sink in golden retreat."

Rallying the Troops

After the Battle with Hamad ina Kamas, Biriir was depleted, badly injured, and exhausted. I sat with him on the starboard keel of the galleon, each of us enclosed in our own bubble but beside one another as comrades. We silently watched the floral corals and the gentle changing hues of the underwater tide. Shoals of fish flitted by turning in spirals and shooting off in all directions flashing silver arrows. I held my hand out to Biriir and he smiled and took it and we stayed like that for a while.

"Does it hurt?" I asked

"A little," he replied. He's not big on words, Biriir ina Barqo, and so we sat in stillness understanding one another's silence.

The warrior Faeries spent that day preparing for our advance to Sector A. Though Biriir was weak, he was to take up position in the front lines of battle and the warrior Faeries would advance behind. We were to be protected, which I was glad about because I didn't want any harm to come to Joe, Uncle Benedict, Buster, or Faras, but I knew that as soon as it was possible, I would depart alone. For the next part of the journey could be completed by me alone. It had been discussed with Queen Qelhatat and agreed.

"If any harm comes to them, the agreement is over," I had said and she had nodded.

"We will protect them as far as we can. The rest is up to you. If you cannot complete your quest then there is no hope."

That's just great, I thought, *no pressure then!*

The Faeries had their own armies and they were a formidable force that made me think we might just have enough power against the Jinn if we caught them off guard.

"Do not underestimate our enemy," Queen Qelhatat had said, "we are powerful but without Nidar, we have little hope."

I understood. "When will the slipstream open again?"

"Within a few days. The planets will realign. You know, your mother was beautiful when I first met her."

This took me by surprise. "How did you come to know her? How did she contact you?"

"A long time ago she first arrived. She was exploring the Sectors. It was not long after she entered that Huur discovered her. He was always searching, rooting through the System, using it in his favor looking for people that might be useful to him. Your mother was a brilliant woman, it didn't take him long to discover her and have her taken to Sector A. She knew how to write code and build the kind of programs he needed to control others. The Corporation used her and then sold her to Huur so that they could keep secret the work she had been doing in building The Gate."

"Didn't she refuse?" I asked.

"Nobody refuses Huur, he has ways of punishing those you love in order to make you do his bidding."

"Huur would've killed you then and your father perhaps or got the Corporation to do it. She did it to protect you."

"But if I am from the Ancients, then my mother must be too, right? She must have come from here?" I asked.

"Your mother is the only one that can tell you about that, child. Let's find her and then all of your questions can be answered."

Why were people always keeping secrets from me? I thought and shook my head.

Overthrow

Vincent stood before Huur in the hall of the great Pyramid. After locating the new Gate he had reset the co-ordinates and used it to access the city.

"And so the Gate works. How did you locate it?" Huur asked.

"We have an inside man, who has been watching the engineer. My father arranged it. We followed him, watched them and eventually traced him through his sister."

"Your father, not you?"

"No," Vincent was embarrassed.

Huur cackled. "I see you, Mister Vincent," he said. "Under the thumb of your father, overpowered by him all of your life, ruled by him. When will you step out from beneath his shadow, I wonder? Are you ruthless enough to do business with? Do you have what it takes to grasp power in your hands and keep its strangle hold?"

"My father does not know I am here," Vincent replied. "I have a proposal for you on my own terms. We can triple the consignment size and ship it out immediately. I have made the arrangements with several countries on Earth that wish to dispose of some, let's just say, undesirable material, that cannot be dumped elsewhere. We have agreed generous terms and they do not wish to know any of the details. That will be our little secret. But you will deal only with me. A phased proposal."

Huur sat back on his throne, his eagle eyes bore deep into Vincent. "That would destroy Sectors C and B and everything on it."

Vincent turned sharply. "Are you getting a conscience, Your Majesty? You have never mentioned one before! From what I understand of you as a businessman, that would not be a problem but if I misunderstood your ruthlessness and desire for power, control and wealth, then do enlighten me further."

"Your understanding of my 'methods' is correct."

"Then my proposal is this, Phase 1, you will remain safe here on Sector A and all of your enemies would be annihilated.

"Phase 2. Use Sector A to dump the latest 'consignment' and come to Earth. Bring the Jinn and your armies. We can command power and a rapid take over. We already have members of the highest governments working for us. I believe it would take only a slight financial incentive for them to see things from our perspective and how advantageous our cause could be to them."

"And if they are not interested in money?"

"Everyone has their price. If they do not want money, we offer them a position. If they do not want power, we convince them how lucky they are to have family and freedom!"

"Your father has underestimated you. When is the consignment due?"

"If you agree, within the next few days."

"Then triple the consignment as you wish and let us begin our own special alliance. But, Mister Vincent, if you cross me in the way that you have done your own people, I will inflict pain upon you that you never imagined existed."

"I would expect little else, Your Majestic Highness."

Yield to the Stars

They had never travelled to Sector A. No one had since the time of the Ancients and the Aayanie when they communed with the spirits and the Jinn. Since then, it was too well-defended, protecting Huur and The System, and very few people apart from Huur's servants knew what happened there or what Huur had done to the planet. There were rumors of ghost armies and creatures that were neither alive nor dead, but they were just rumors and the real situation was closely guarded by Huur and his servants. We needed to be prepared for anything.

And so, we gathered in the place where we had, just a few days before, arrived on Sector B where the slipstream had landed us. A fleet of magnificent old galleon ships risen from the ocean bed with their great masts and white sails like the bellies of giant whales, lined up along the shore of the Sa'ad ad Din islands with the army of warrior Faeries armed and ready for battle. The breeze blew strong and the air rippled above us as the slipstream blew in on the wind. One by one the ships began to tilt upward, as though picked up by an invisible hand. Rising up ship by ship with full sails, we were carried toward an uncertain fate.

Joe and I stood at the bow of the ship watching the giant red planet looming before us. It looked alive and turbulent with erupting volcanoes and if a planet can be described as angry, then it was raging and in full fury.

"Do you think Kareem is there?" asked Joe.

"I hope so, Joe, we have to believe that he is, that all of this has not been for nothing," I replied gently.

"And your mother?"

"And my mother too."

Uncle Benedict stood beside the Warrior Queen Qelhatat. "Will they be waiting for us?" he asked.

"Almost certainly," she replied. "Huur knows everything, he has eyes everywhere. The Cube will have already alerted him when we left Sector B."

"And who will be our welcoming committee?"

"That is unknown. We have not been able, in the same way to gain knowledge of Huur's army and it is certain there will be one. He is the most hated and loathed figure in the Sectors and has made many enemies. He will be heavily protected. It is possible that none of us will return."

They looked at one another.

"And the children?" Uncle Benedict said.

"We must protect them, especially the girl, even if it means losing our lives, for without her, there is no future for us. She does not know her powers, her strength, and has not begun to use them but once she does, there is no telling what she might achieve."

I tried to keep my eyes open, force myself awake but with the gentle rocking of the ship on the Slipstream, Joe and I sat and drifted into a deep sleep.

When I woke up at Uncle Benedict's, Mister Vincent was sitting in a chair, waiting for me and with him was Mr Shah.

An Escape of Two

The door to Kareem's prison slid quietly open.

"You must be quick," Amel said. "When they find out you have gone, they will come for me."

"Where are you? What must I do?"

"Don't concern yourself about me. It's Aya that matters. Keep her safe."

"But how? She could be anywhere by now."

"She is coming to Sector A but is in grave danger. The Corporation are planning a huge disposal of toxic waste any time now."

"How do you know this?" asked Kareem.

"Everything is done through the System. It is all recorded. I have secured your release. Ayaa will arrive at the Mountain of Angels. You must make sure she gets there and speaks with Nidar. Search for the Mountain of Angels, be quick."

At that the screen shut down and Amel was gone. "Well, Cube, looks like we have a mission on our hands. Turn on sat nav and get us out of here. We have a job to do. Real life levels where the consequences could mean actual death."

"I understand, Kareem. Glad to see you back in the game," Cube replied.

They left the cell and entered into a dimly lit corridor. Passing other cells, some empty some occupied with strange looking creatures, Kareem passed one and then paused and returned. The video screen outside the cell showed an elderly, Muslim woman. Could it be?

"Cube, check identity on the prisoner in that cell." Cube did an A.I search and confirmed Fatima's identity.

"If you try to release her, Kareem, we may be discovered," Cube said.

Kareem sighed. "I can't leave her here, Cube, she's an old woman, anything could be in store for her. I'd never forgive myself. Help me find a way to open the cell door."

"Kareem it cannot be opened from outside."

"There must be a way. How did Amel get our door open?"

She changed the code programming on the door release.

"Then let's do that, can we do that?"

"I will have to enter the central system. It may take a few moments."

Seconds felt like hours before the lock clicked open. Kareem ran in, much to the surprise of Fatima who stood up in alarm.

Kareem stood there smiling. "Come on, we're leaving. This is a rescue mission."

Fatima wasted no time as she followed Kareem from the cell and they made their way through the chambers, "Then I will consider myself rescued. What's the plan?"

"We have to find Amel, Aya's mother. I can't leave without her, it would be wrong."

"And then?"

"We find you a place of safety and I find Aya. Cube, get us out of here."

Larks and Thieves

"Who is this?" I asked Mr Shah, cautiously looking for my nearest means of escape. "Why did you betray my parents? They trusted you, we all trusted you. Don't think I haven't figured it out. How you set up the whole thing."

"Now, now Aya, don't be ungrateful." Mr Vincent replied. There was something about him, something too immaculate, too neat, too controlled. He was sitting in the chair with his foot on one knee, his hands together forming an arch, in his pin stripped suit and I was reminded somehow of that stormy night when Mr Shah had come to our house and this whole thing had begun.

"You don't need to know who I am, Aya, you just need to tell me what I want to know and then we can all go our separate ways, can't we." Mr Vincent smiled but it was not the smile of a happy man and it was not a question but a command.

"What is it you need to know from me then?" I asked.

"Well, we need to know the whereabouts of your Uncle Benedict and," he sighed, "of your mother who appears to be missing."

"I can't help you," I replied, "though if I could I wouldn't."

"Now, now, Aya, don't be unkind. You have knowledge of her, that's why you went there, isn't it, in the first place?"

"What do you mean? Went where?"

"To the other world. You went because your mother called you."

He knew a lot, too much, he must be from the Corporation. But how did he know that I'd entered the world and that my mother had called me to it? Even I hadn't known that.

"I see from your expression that you are surprised. Did you know that your mother had called you in?" He was studying my face in a way that made me feel very uncomfortable.

"Ahhh, you didn't. So you haven't found her yet. Then I'm premature in my arrival. A word of advice, never trust your parents, Aya. That mother of yours has put you in grave danger, hmmm."

I said nothing. Suddenly, in the silent moment between us, his phone rang. Answering it, he stood up and his demeanor changed.

His voice was cold as he demanded of Mr Shah "Watch her," and he left the small house that somehow felt too warm and soft for his presence.

"Aya, did you find him?" Mr Shahs urgent whisper came as a surprise. "Kareem. Is he there? You must tell me child, quickly before Vincent returns."

For a moment I was confused, unable to think clearly. How would Mr Shah know about Kareem? Why would he be looking for......? And then I saw it, what had been obvious all along and I looked into the face of a man with silver hair, older than Kareem with the eyes, not of someone who was devious and manipulative, but the eyes of someone who had grieved and lost like me.

"Kareem is your son," I said with certainty.

"He was just a small child when he had the accident. Since then he has been asleep, in a coma many people call it. Everyone said, 'give up you will never have your son back' but I know that he is there, somewhere. My son still exists in spirit, I know it."

"Your son still exists, very much in spirit," I laughed.

Mr Shah leapt up and took my hands in his. "I knew it. I knew that someday, someone would find him. I have been looking for so long now, hoping and praying."

"But how did you know it would be me?" I asked.

"I didn't know. How could I? When I heard stories, rumors about the other world, I infiltrated the Corporation, began working for them. Since then it has become my life. There were a few leads, families who had loved ones taken, disappeared, and so I went to them, just as I did with you and your father, gave them opportunities in order to follow them and report back to the Corporation. But with one aim in my mind; to find my son. To find him in the other world."

We talked conspiratorially in whispers for a few moments, watching for Mr Vincent's impending return. Mr Shah told me of the terrible road accident that Kareem suffered as a child that left him in a permanent sleeping state and, in return, I spoke of how wonderful a friend Kareem had become and his life in Moonlight.

As suddenly, as it had begun, our conversation was interrupted abruptly by the return of Mr Vincent who now looked angrier than ever. That phone conversation could not have gone very well because his face had turned as red as a Lobster.

"Well, if you find your mother or your uncle returns," he placed a card on the oak desk by the window, "you will know how to contact me, won't you, Aya. And you will contact me. We wouldn't want anything terrible happening to your father or his new wife, would we?" With that threat, he turned and left.

Mr Shah, stood and followed Mr Vincent but before he walked out the door he turned and gave a small nod.

I heard the roar of a car engine and rushed to the door to see their chauffer driven car disappear down the driveway. Did they know about the Gate? If so, how much time did we have before the Corporation took it to be used for their own ends. And if they did, what would happen to Joe, Uncle Benedict, and Buster? They would be trapped forever in Moonlight! I wondered too, if Kareem would ever be able to return.

I had to do something. I had to end all of this and fast.

Leaving

Deep below ground, beneath Huurs Great Pyramid, a network of tunnels connected the Central Programming rooms for The System. Behind miles of corridors, stood miles of doors. Behind miles of doors sat imprisoned workers who manipulated and changed a million screens and game levels. Anyone living in the Sectors was tracked.

My mother sat in a small chamber, isolated, writing code for new and increasingly complex games levels. The harder the level, the greater the distraction and that meant fewer people watching Huur.

She had also been given another, more ominous task; to detect and report anyone off grid. It was possible, using the navigation systems to recognize authorised citizens. If a person was not in The System, they could be found but not identified. Huur did not like this and would send out his minions to locate and capture anyone not registered.

There was also the matter of the Warrior Faeries who were very hard to track because they lived in the sea.

At the same time she had secretly tapped into and was watching the surveillance cameras operating in the Dungeon cells. It had not been easy getting into the security systems and had put her life in danger but she had managed it. She watched now as Kareem stalled outside the cell of Fatima and she worked quickly to override the alarm system for the locking code to the door which Cube was, at this very moment, trying to break into.

She had intervened already without anyone's knowledge, using The System to call into my dreams, changing the levels in our favour to send us allies, showing me signs and sending us Moonlight when we most needed her.

Amal watched as the door released open and Kareem and Fatima made their urgent escape. She blocked the cameras from The System but it was already beginning to suspect an unauthorised intervention.

An alarm ran out echoing through the corridors, "Malfunction in software," a flat computer voice said. "Emergency detection of malfunction required. All agents will comply with emergency detection."

"Where is Amal?" Kareem asked Fatima.

Fatima stopped and stood completely still with her eyes closed.

"Er, what are you doing?" asked Kareem. "This is a bit, urgent, we need to leave right now." The alarm was ringing all around the great pyramid.

Fatima raised her hand. "Wait, I am listening."

"What to?" asked Kareem.

"To The System," Fatima replied calmly.

"We need to leave immediately Kareem, we have been detected," Cube stated.

"I can hear her, feel her presence," Fatima said. She opened her eyes and moved swiftly in the direction they had come. "This way, quickly."

Kareem rushed after her. "I hope you know what you are doing. What was that, back there?"

"I have some powers," Fatima replied, "some Aayanie ancestry. But it is weak and this conversation is not for now. Quick, this way."

Amal realized that Kareem and Fatima were coming to release her. She had to decide, after years of imprisonment and slavery to Huur, was it better to risk everything in escape or stay put and try to help the others?

Suddenly, an unwelcome face appeared on the computer screen. "Miss Amal, your presence is sincerely requested in the Temple." Huur did not sound sincere. Far from it, he sounded menacing.

Amal completed one last action, and then she ran.

Halicarnassus

Nobody could tell me what lay ahead. This could only be done alone. Desperately wishing I could say goodbye, to thank the others for their love and companionship, I knew I had to leave without those farewells because they would only insist on coming with me. It was decided in my discussion with Queen Qelhatat that I would have a better chance if I took the Coracle and slipped away unnoticed. All of Huur's energies and attention would be drawn toward the Fleet and with a small chance, my absence might go undetected.

Joe opened his eyes. "What are you doing?" he whispered.

"I'm sorry, Joe," I replied sadly.

"Go get 'em," he said and reached into his pocket and handed his catapult to me. A little sob left me as I ruffled his hair.

"Stay safe Joe," I whispered climbing into *Moonlight,* "I will come back, I will find you."

I never felt so alone as in that moment when the Coracle sailed away on the slipstream toward an unknown destiny.

We flew low over the planet. I was scared I don't mind telling you and hoped my leaving had not been detected by Huur. The surface looked thunderous and angry, grey and dark with occasional bursts of molten fire. I didn't know where I was going so I scanned looking for clues. Queen Qelhatat had said '*Look for the Mountain of Angels*' but the planet was so vast, how was I to know where to find it?

Just then, as if by magic, a small blue bird flew alongside me. It flitted up, under and over *Moonlight* and I recognized it from the Cave of Shimberaale on Sector C. I leaned into *Moonlight* and we followed it as it wove its way toward, what looked like, a ruined city on the surface of the planet.

We set down in an old square in the shadow of a giant metropolis. Did the spirits once live here and if so, they must have been giants like Habbad and Biriir, titans of their times. I felt so small, so insignificant, like an ant that could be snuffed out in the blink of an eye.

The city was deserted *Where should I start?*

"Come on, girl, you are here to do a job," I persuaded myself trying to gain courage. "What did Queen Qelhatat say—look for the Legendary View. Well, what does that mean, all of this is legendary, seriously the instructions could be a bit better, I have to save all of humanity and an instruction manual would be really useful at this point."

The city was too vast. I could walk for weeks, months and not find what I was looking for, or simply walk right by it. Ahead a few miles away, I could see a hill rising up with a view that would allow me to see the city. I hurried toward it trying not to think about there being anything around that could harm me, like ghosts or Jinn or Jinn-ghosts or giant robots or very, very angry pharaohs!

As I climbed up the steep hill, I could see the city in all its glory. Like the ruins of Athens, a place of beauty that had once been occupied but now had become so desolate. I imagined it bustling with giants like the old cities I had heard of in history lessons in school. And now there were only ruins. Casting my eye across the city landscape, one of the buildings stood out more than others. It was a huge place of worship like the Aya Sofia in Istanbul, something between a Masjid and a Cathedral, and it dominated the city.

Now that looks like a place for a Legendary View, I thought. Clambering back down the hill, I marched off the through eerie streets with great fallen monuments covered in clambering creepers.

Reaching the foot of the steps, I gazed upward and marveled at its timelessness. "Come on, Aya," I urged myself, "people are depending on you."

Undertaking the Final Battle

Huur's army stood in geometric lines, in their thousands. A huge grid, stretching for miles. Like a wall of terror they had stood motionless, awaiting the arrival of the warriors from Sector B. Chalk white bodies glowed from the light of the flames that seeped up through the black crevices of molten lava underneath their soulless bodies. Their faces, masks without expression painted red and black. They stood like clay, unmoving, frozen.

They too were Ancients, existing before the final creation of the planets, but they had been taken, held, and changed by poisons seeping into their food, water, and soil and then the final imprisonment when Huur had kept them in darkness until all humanity had left them and they had become unevolved from their nature and could only speak to the dark Jinn. Like a plague they had grown but unlike the Jinn, they had not evolved intelligence and existed only to serve violence. That is all they lived for and their entire purpose now.

Vincent, Hunt, and Huur stood on the balcony of Huur's great Pyramid fortress surveying all of Huur's army spread out below.

"And so the consignment of radioactive material has arrived on Sector B just as they make their way to you. How fortuitous," laughed Hunt. "If they do ever get to return, they will find Sectors C and B in pretty poor shape. Better for them if you finish them off here." Vincent had set up the deal but Hunt had claimed the glory for himself as usual.

"This is a mighty army," Hunt continued. And then to his son, "Look what you can achieve if you are ruthless enough!"

"You have my payment?" asked Huur.

"Vincent, fetch the bag," Hunt ordered his son, who picked up a large bag and dropped it in front of Huur. "I think you'll find that satisfactory, everything we agreed. Count it if you like."

"No need," Huur replied. "You would never be foolish enough to try and cheat me. The consequences would be too severe!" Grabbing hold of the payment Huur strode inside. "Deposit this in the vault," he commanded his servant.

Vincent walked in from the balcony alone, a few moments later. Huur asked in surprise, "Your father is not joining us?" Vincent looked up and sighed. "Such a shame, a terrible accident. Tragically he leaned too close to the edge and there was simply nothing I could do to save him! However, he died as he would have wanted, in battle."

"Huur grinned in approval. I do believe that you are becoming someone I can do business with now the problem to your success has been removed."

Black Ravens screamed, darting flocks crossing the sky swooping low to join the army as they began to awaken.

High above from the Heavens, galleons appeared carrying their great winged passengers in front of the moon like avenging spirits journeying towards fate.

At Huur's command, the army turned and marched out to meet them on the dark plains that stretched before the Pyramid. The battle was about to begin.

"You must stay here," Uncle Benedict said to Joe and Faras. "You will be watched over and kept safe. Do you understand? You must not leave the safety of the ship."

"Yes," said Joe. He and Faras nodded. Joe had absolutely no intention of staying put and as soon as he was able, to escape his protector, he was going to join in the battle, no matter how fierce and frightening it might be.

"What about Buster?"

Uncle Benedict looked down at his old friend who was watching him with a knowing wizened look. "Buster and I have fighting to do, don't we, old boy?" And then, they left with the others, marching toward a sinister and terrifying army overlooked by a more sinister Pyramid shining golden against a setting sun.

"Kareem and Aya are doing their bit," Joe whispered to Faras, "we will do ours." Faras agreed.

The Warrior Faeries, looked resplendent and fearless in spirit, on the move with Queen Qelhatat taking lead.

"They look formidable, Faras," Joe said, "I wouldn't want to be on the receiving end of their fury. Come on, let's join at the back and try to keep your antennae down." But the army was so numerous that it was a long time before Joe and Faras could fall in unobserved, ducking and diving behind rocks and low flying Faeries.

From two sides of the valley the armies marched meeting at the center of the flat plateau of desolate land. The earth cracked and shook under foot as they approached. They came to a halt facing one another. In between plumes of smoke and fire crept up from the ground, hissing and spitting. Queen Qelhatat marched out to meet Huur in the space between the two armies. The air buzzed with anxious anticipation.

Halting just meters away from Huur, her golden wings shone in effervescence as fire flowed from the live volcanoes in the hills behind.

"Free the Sectors, Huur, and stop selling off our planets for the dumping of poisonous waste. Meet these demands and we will leave you and your armies unharmed."

Huur's menacing smile turned to mocking laughter, a laughter of his disdain. Queen Qelhatat knew with certainty that Huur would show no concern or love for his people for their lives or deaths. Not now, not ever.

"You come to my land, making demands, asking for leniency? Now, now, Faerie Queen, what do you really hope to gain? What kind of a leader marches their people into certain death?"

"It is not your land, Huur, you have stolen it. The Sectors never belonged to you, just as no tribal leader owned the lands or their people. Make no mistake, we will take back the lands and restore them to their original condition that nature intended. I have endured the screaming and the pain of the planets under your oppression long enough."

She had offered him a way out of what was about to happen. She had eased her conscience and done her duty by the Ancients, looking for the right path. Now, regrettably, there would be battle, blood, and death.

He began talking, mocking her and her people but she knew that listening to him now was futile. She turned away, lifted her mighty wings and flew back to her people. As she approached them she tilted her head giving the order and they raised their weapons, raised their heads, raised their wings, and charged toward the enemy.

Huur's wings stretched to their full might. Watching the Queen turn away from him, he let out a loud roar of rage, a war cry that echoed out across the plains enraging his terrible army that, in unison, marched forward in lines.

"Kill them, kill them all!" he cried.

The red earth thundered beneath the movement of a thousand bodies. One face, one movement but all under his command.

The first wave clashed and enmeshed in a fit of bodies, weapons, and screams like a hellish dance of wrestling rolling, diving and falling. Some fell, some rose. The Jinn came in on the next wave splitting into sections and creeping into the hearts and souls of the Faeries, devouring them with tortured thoughts and waking nightmares. Actions seemed to appear in slow motion as lives were taken without mercy.

Uncle Benedict threw himself at the enemy with laser Cube and sword drawn, Buster by his side, snarling, biting, and dragging the ghosts to the ground. Beside them Biriir stormed into dozens of the chalk army, slaying them with his bare hands and breaking their bodies, thrashing them to the ground. Armed with Cubes of energy and swords, the Faeries and Queen Qelhatat fired at the Jinn or cut them down, slaying a path through them, moving with intent, making her way toward Huur.

Joe and Faras were partially hidden behind rocks, watching the battle unfold. "We need to protect Uncle

Benedict, Biriir and Buster," Joe said to Faras who whinnied in agreement. It was hard to see through the malay of wings, and turbulent activity but Biriir could be seen standing heads high above the others.

"There he is, let's move in." And as Joe and Faras rushed towards Biriir they caught sight of a line of Jinn stealthy creeping up on Uncle Benedict, knocking him to the ground. Buster was barking and snapping at them but they were too formidable.

"Quick, Faras, charge!" Joe shouted, galloping toward the impending disaster as fast as Faras' trotters could carry them. Holding his Cube high and like a cavalry, Joe fired into the circling Jinn using it like a machine gun, cutting into the line and splitting the Jinn in half. The few valuable seconds of ambush and surprise were enough for Buster and Uncle Benedict to retreat, gain composure, and fire back at the Jinn once more splitting and depleting their power.

Suddenly the Jinn stopped and turned away. Huur had called them. "The girl, he commanded, you must find the girl!"

Mighty Nidar Awakens

The Citadel was higher than the tallest building I had ever seen. Rising almost into the clouds, its ceiling all but disappeared. Ancient writing, like hieroglyphs, were written on the walls, in beautiful pictures; a language I had never seen and could not translate but one made me think of nature and music. Shafts of light came in through broken windows and climbing clematis and ivy trailed the walls. Those little blue tropical birds appeared again, in the dusk and I wondered how they came to be there. Apart from the flutter of wings against the air, this place was silent. It was the same silence I'd known after my mother had gone, as though the whole world had stopped existing but this was calm, and that had not been.

I walked up to a central pedestal and felt the warmth of light beams upon my skin. I had been a child then, but I knew the words of Queen Qelhatat had been correct. She had always been there with me, in my heart, my memory. I'd banished the real thought of her somewhere because I didn't want to feel alone, abandoned, angry, and I knew then that I may always feel those things. I stood there knowing that it was alright to feel sadness and that it wouldn't destroy me. With closed eyes, I listened, smelled the scent of the flowers and the dry dust that floated in the air, the solid earth under my feet.

The light faded golden and still only the birds stirred. I waited. Then I heard them. The voices. Sounds that seemed to come from within me. Looking back now, I can't tell you who they were, those that spoke with me. Perhaps they were part of a game, The System, or maybe some Ancient tribe that nobody knew existed. Perhaps they never existed at all, but I heard them, I talked with them in that ancient lost language used by Ayaanie for the first time and they helped me.

"She is not ready," said a soft female voice.

I am ready, I replied in thought as sunlight fell onto my face. Though it was natural and gentle, it seemed to be searching.

"Perhaps we should let the child try," the first voice said.

"Perhaps we should," agreed another, "she is Ayaanie after all."

"Child, what is it you seek?"

At this all of my thoughts occurred in my mind at once like voices layered over one another or thinking without full sentences. *My mother, Nidar, must help Queen Qelhatat, Joe, save Joe. They lied to me. Faras abandoned, in the cells the dungeons Kareem, believing me. I'm not who they think.*

"You must concentrate child, slowly, one thought at a time. Concentrate on the words only, as you would if you were speaking."

I took a deep breath and calmed myself imagining a book in front of me, a letter, reading from it. My thoughts slowed and became clearer.

I must speak with Nidar.

"There are few that can do so. Nidar sleeps very deeply and has not spoken with another for many years. What is it you want to say, child?"

Huur is destroying the planet, killing off the Sectors and enslaving people. Only Nidar has the power to stop him, he is too strong.

"But that is not all you come for, is it? You are searching for something."

I took a deep breath. "I need to know who I am," I said and it felt real and I understood.

Silence followed but it didn't matter. Whatever happened next I knew that all that mattered was within reach.

"Go to the Mountain of Angels, child, take your message to Nidar in the sea of fire. On the cliffs you will call but beware, it is dangerous to speak with the Ancient Spirits."

Is it far? I replied in thought.

"Have no fear in that, child, you are not alone."

Just then, like an avenging angel, a beautiful white horse appeared from somewhere high above. There was somebody riding it. I shielded my eyes against the light. Then a familiar voice rang out.

"Hey, nice outfit, you look like a boy! Better than being on an adventure in your pajamas I suppose!"

"Kareeeem," I shouted as he landed and ran toward him, throwing my arms around him in a huge hug. The horse was so powerful and strong, pure white, almost glowing in the half-light but with strong, brave wings, large enough to carry the weight of its muscular body. It was a Pegasus.

"It is good to see you again," Cube said politely.

"You too Cube," I replied and I really meant it.

"I see you've mastered horse riding Kareem. Faras will be impressed!" I laughed. "Let me look at you, are you OK? What did they do to you, Kareem?"

"Jump up and I'll tell you everything on the way," he replied. "I believe we have a few planets and a couple of worlds to save!"

Without hesitation, I jumped up onto the Pegasus and held tightly to Kareem. We flew out of the Citadel, low just over the rooftops of the incredible ruined city and ahead, a long way ahead on the horizon I could just make out a slither of fire that I knew must be the sea we were looking for.

"Up ahead is the sea of fire," Cube said with authority.

The Pegasus flew down, landing on a cliff top at the edge of the sea. Beyond, we could see a group of islands toward the horizon. Just visible was a peak jutting up higher than the rest.

"Cube, can you locate the Mountain of Angels?" I asked.

"I am sorry to be a disappointment, Aya but that is an Ancient name and does not appear in my system," Cube replied.

"What do you think," Kareem said, pointing out to the islands, "does that look like a Mountain of Angels to you?"

"It could be," I replied, the island before of us was shaped in the form of a caldera, with a volcanic island at its heart. Steam rose from it and drifted across the ocean. "Let's take a closer look."

As we went, I updated Kareem with everything that had happened since we were parted, of finding Uncle Benedict and Buster, meeting Biriir, Queen Qelhatat, the slip stream and the Faerie Warriors on Sector B. In return, he told me of the terrible encounter with Huur and the Jinn and how scared he was but how he pretended not to be. He told me of Huur's plan to lure me to the dungeons using him and my mother as bait and about my mother rescuing him.

"Kareem, there is something very important that I haven't said, something you must know," I spoke as we landed on a ledge on the side of the volcanic island. It was as good a spot and gave us a view of most of the mountain and the small island below. I did not know how he would react but I had to tell him everything. He listened intently and sat down, knees pulled into his chest looking out across the sea. We sat in silence for a while.

"So, I have a family. I'm a boy, from your world?"

"From our world Kareem," I replied.

"What are they like, my parents?"

"Your father I think is a good man Kareem, and you look a lot alike. Your mother must be too. They've been through a lot to find you and they never gave up. If you decide to come back with me, they'll be there." He was still looking very thoughtful.

I added, "and my mother, is she safe, my mother?"

"Yes, Cube and I released your mother and Fatima. She said she knew a place of safety where they could hide and led me to the Pegasus. There are many Ancient animals from Sector C, held by Huur in captivity. Peg was lucky to survive." He patted the beautiful creature and she reared up stretching her wings out, enjoying her freedom. "Fatima said you would be in the Citadel."

I told Kareem about the Legendary View. "There is a shape that it fits, only one place in this world and at only one time."

"But why," he asked, "would you need a puzzle to awaken a spirit and why only a certain time and place?"

"I think the puzzle, it's like a transformer Kareem that connects me to Nidar. On Earth we have animals that hibernate into deep sleep. I think Nidar is a bit like that. Soon she will be awake enough to hear me, but only if we get this right and only if I can actually speak with her in the ancient language."

"And can you?" he asked with raised eyebrows?

"I don't know Kareem, truly, I don't" I replied solemnly. In my hand were three images that looked like a code with lines and slots. I took out the map that had been given to me. They could be an ancient mask if looked at closely but had no outlines. "Queen Qelhatat said that I would be able to read this, to look for the clues but I cannot see how that is possible. I think she places too much faith in me." I said quickly. I looked around but there were no clues, it felt hopeless and impossible.

"And how do we know when the time is right?" Kareem asked?

"I don't know that either but if Huur is searching for my mother and Fatima and you, and if the others have begun the battle, then we must work quickly or we will be too late for any of this to make a difference. We must be looking for a sign."

"Let me have a look at that, I'm a pro at games, remember?" He turned the puzzle pieces over in his hands, inspecting them carefully. "I think I know this one. I've seen something like it in the levels though this is far more complicated. They look separate but you have to fit them into a kind of jigsaw and overlap them at angles. The problem is you have to do it in the right place and that can take time."

"It looks really dangerous out there, Kareem," I replied, watching the fire and heat rising up from the sea all around the island.

"It is," he smiled. "You didn't think that saving the world would be easy, did you? Come on, let's do this and get us all back home with our families, where we belong."

We jumped onto the Pegasus together, holding tightly onto the puzzle pieces.

The lava around the island did not behave in the way you would have expected. It leapt and swung and danced. It twisted and pounced unexpectedly upward and sideways. We flew away from it, giving it space. And there, set deep into the mountainside was a landing, almost entirely hidden.

"There, just like in the dream, Kareem, it was in the dream all along!" I shouted. "I've been here before!"

'Find the place and the correct time.' Queen Qelhatat had said. I had already known it. The Pegasus moved us in toward the small opening, carefully trying to keep her balance as she neared the edge of the cliff and molten lava spewed up all around us. The temperature was beginning to rise as we landed at the steps of the staircase.

"It's all about signs and symbols and clues when you are in the game," Kareem replied. "The answer is obvious when you know what you are looking for."

The staircase spiralled upwards into the mountain for ages, becoming narrower and darker but I knew that somewhere near the top, the Legendary View was there. Breathlessly, we climbed until we reached a small opening. We entered a room with walls the colour of moonlight. It shone with an ethereal glow that took my breath away and although the walls appeared to be there, like a TARDIS, they expanded outwards into a space beyond the mountain, beyond the planet, beyond the stars. And there, suspended in mid-air in the centre of this place that defied all the laws of science and space, was the thing I had been seeking.

Two miniature universes rotated side by side surrounded by planets, nebulae and stars, some were familiar and others that could only be guessed at. We could not know if this was a map, a projection, or if it was real.

Kareem gasped. "If this isn't a legendary view, Aya, then I don't know what is!"

Is this why the spirits were here on this island? Why they had always been here? Is this what they were protecting? I believed it was. The greatest treasure in existence, protected by the strongest and most ancient of the spirits.

"The pieces," said Kareem urgently.

I took them from my pocket. There was no time to lose as the planets turned on their axis and seemed to be moving toward an alignment.

"It must be to do with the alignment of the planets," Kareem said. "I'm looking for an overlap, they may not sit perfectly. Can you see the shadow of Sector C being cast over Sector B? The same thing must be occurring here."

"I'm not sure. The light is moving so fast," I said, looking out through a small window in the cave overlooking the ocean. We rotated around and around the planets. "Here," I shouted, "underneath!" Kareem placed one of the pieces underneath the universe and it hovered in the air.

"That's the trick," said Kareem, "move the pieces where you see the curved lines of the planets, match the slots and see where they want to fit. When they hover we will know they are in the right place."

So that's what we did and as each piece found its place, an alignment in our universe began between all of the planets in the Sectors.

So, we stood, waiting, praying, and looking for the last piece as the shadow cast by the planets fell over the pieces in the small universe before us and externally in the universe outside. And as they rotated, I knew the pieces of the puzzle were alive. Suddenly, something powerful had entered the room. It was the Jinn. The light vanished leaving us in darkness.

"Kareem, I'm scared." I said, stepping back towards the staircase.

"Wait, you can do this," he said reassuringly, "it's almost over." Kareem stood between The Jinn and me as I began lifting the final piece into place. My arms trembled and felt so heavy, I could not move them. Something was creeping into my lungs and I struggled to breathe. There was nothing Kareem could do to stop them.

There was a growing intensity around us as the darkness of the Jinn reached into my lungs and began to suffocate me, an invisible power shook the room like a force field. The pieces solidified for a moment, heavy and light, all at once, creating an image of a face. It opened its eyes and looked at us. An electrical movement erupted across the miniature planet that was sector A and through the air into the cave, and we knew that what was happening in front of us, was happening across the planet outside the cave too.

The Jinn reared up. I swung around, trying to escape. The A molten sea raged outside like a charging bull. The Jinn tightened its grip on my lungs. The power of its height and impact was paralyzing. I wanted to run, to take Kareem's hand and fly away on the Pegasus, but we could never have outrun it. I had to finish what I had begun even if it meant losing my life, I had to finish it. I stood up holding the last piece, the wave was before me now and death was almost certain. The Jinn blocked out everything now in slow motion, filled my vision. Tears ran down my face as I turned to Kareem. "I'm sorry," I tried to say but no words came. With my last breathe, I held up the last piece as darkness came to crush me, the tiny beautiful universe, Kareem and the Pegasus with the weight and power of its hatred. I held the piece up before this last image and I did not flinch, I did not turn away. I surrendered.

Although we did not see Nidar, we felt her all around us like electricity, like life itself. She encompassed me and I felt her reading my thoughts, her power like a softness, like water pressing into my mind, trickling into every part of my memory, not to invade but to find something and I felt heavy and light at the same time. Kareem stood before me shouting, trying to take my hand, to pull me away from the Jinn, but I could hear and feel nothing, just the sensation of being held, lifted up. And then, in a flash, she was gone. My body dropped to the ground. A force swept out from me, sending shock waves across the room, wiping out the Jinn and everything in its path.

For a moment there was complete stillness. The shock wave rippled outward across the planets, across the solar system like an electrical current. It could not be seen as such but its path swept through every living thing, every molecule destroying anything poisonous on impact.

I felt Nidar's power and it was devastating. Devastating, that is to all things that were not of benefit to the planet and to its nature. On the battlefield, they felt the wave too, raw positive energy, felt it move through them across the space between the sectors and on toward sector B. In a split second Huur's army was annihilated. His Pyramid, the center of his entire reign where he had wielded so much destruction and power, was wiped out, flattened in a breath. The Jinn had not even had time to scream.

Watching from our small space on sector A, we could see the wave of its movement reach the planets on our miniature universe and move around its surface. We could see the brightness of where it had been as the seas sparkled and the islands glowed brighter as if everything had recharged. We could see it move on to sector C where new growth sprouted up, where dark patches diminished and where parts of the red desert changed from dark reds to amber.

It was like watching a miracle of nature.

A Showdown

Meanwhile, on the Battlefield, the Warrior Faeries had been taking out the enemy in great numbers. They were advancing uncomfortably close to Huur's Pyramid base and slaying many more of his army than he had believed possible. Queen Qelhatat regrouped the Faeries, sectioning them into troops, sending some forward and advancing others to surround the enemy from the rear and break them down into manageable units. Another troop were sent around the sides essentially surrounding the enemy and causing groups to be splintered. Huur had retreated back to the safety of Pyramid leaving his army to fight without a leader. He wanted to enjoy the spectacle of his army slaughtering the Warrior Faeries from the safety of his balcony.

Viewing the scene below, it was becoming increasingly clear that Queen Qelhatat and the Faeries were gaining the upper hand.

"How are they succeeding?" Huur asked Vincent. "We have the might, the power, and the strength and we are greater in numbers."

"They believe they are right, and she is a formidable commander of her people," Vincent replied, "they have *morality* on their side. There is something to be learned from watching people fight for a cause. It gives them *inner strength*."

"Then I must use everything in my power to destroy those despicable traits once and for all," Huur sighed. "I am becoming very, very, bored with all of this," he gestured toward the battlefield. "At first it was fun but they are not playing my game and so, the level must end."

A siren call echoed out across the plains, halting some of the skirmishes as everyone turned around. It was impossible to say what Huur had in store for them now.

Electricity filled the air, clouds of thunder rolled toward the plains and lightning struck down from the distant hills.

Everyone froze. The worst thing imaginable rose up from behind the hills, in lines, Giant Dhegdheer, dozens of them captured by Huur from the Emerald Jungle and turned into mutants. They were cloaked in armor made from the waste metals delivered by Vincent and now formed a terrifying army of indestructible and vicious creatures. At Huur's command, an electrical charge sent static sparks through the armor making the fearsome creatures move forward. At first it was with a slow prowl, but gradually they ran faster toward the paralyzed Warrior Faeries who were ill equipped to combat the might such a force presented. Fear trickled all across the plains and people began to run. The crazed laughter of Huur could be heard echoing across the landscape.

Joe and Faras crouched low to the ground, watching these terrifying monsters loom into view on the battlefield. Formidable and indestructible, they electrified the air.

Queen Qelhatat signaled to her army to regroup. Uncle Benedict shouted out to her, "What are those hellish things?"

"I have never seen anything of the like before," she replied, somewhat shaken.

"How do we bring them down?" he replied.

"I do not know but we will find a way. Take the boy, find Huur's Gate in the Pyramid. There is no more you can do here." And with that, she charged toward the Dhegdheer who were already tearing into her people.

Uncle Benedict knew she was right. He must save Joe. Weaving his way through the enemy and the battles, he saw Joe and Faras ahead and to the left battling a particularly gruesome member of Huurs army. It had raised its weapon and was just about to bring it down upon the head of Faras when Uncle Benedict charged it, knocking it off balance. Joe lay injured on the ground. With one move Uncle Benedict raised Joe to his feet, jumped onto the back of Faras, pulled Joe up and raced them away to safety.

Biriir, watched as they made their way toward the Pyramid. He ran forward to place himself in the way of enemies that might try to attack. It was a long and dangerous journey but Biriir held off attack as they swerved in and out of the fighting and beneath the frame of the terrible giant Dhegdheer. The ground grew treacherous underfoot with the fighting. Steam and volcanic rock broke through the surface making visibility poor.

The Pyramid loomed up before them as they charged onwards and the entrance was in sight leaving a clear path. "Go," Biriir shouted, "I will protect you and hold off any advance." He turned to face the enemy.

"Be careful Biriir, stay safe," Joe shouted.

Biriir turned to see them go and just in that moment, as if from nowhere, a Dhegdheer pounced, taking him by surprise. Biriir lunged back at it. Sparks and teeth thrashed as he threw his weight on top of the monster, pressing it down into the ground in a crushing maneuver.

"No!" Joe cried out, breaking free and trying to run back to help Biriir.

Uncle Benedict swung back, grabbed hold of Joe and maneuvered back toward the Pyramid.

"There is nothing we can do, Joe, you must understand that, we would all be killed."

"But it will kill him," Joe was sobbing now.

"He is a brave warrior and has saved our lives. That is how brave warriors wish to die, in the battlefield. Do you think he would want you to risk your life, to die out there? Or remember him as the Giant he was, the warrior that he was? Come on, Joe, let's not make his sacrifice for nothing, let's go home, get you back to others who are waiting for you, who also love you."

Faras' antennae lit up and she whinnied as they entered the chamber arch of the Pyramid. They were in a low-lit antichamber surrounded by hieroglyphics with three passageways, one ahead and the others to the left and right.

Joe wiped his tears. "I think Faras knows the way," he said shakily

"Then let's follow her and hope that she does," said Uncle Benedict ruffling Joe's hair.

Outside the battle raged on but now the tide was turning in the favor of the Dheghdeer and Huur.

Below ground the corridors were numerous and maze like but at ground level and above they were well lit with high passages steeped in golden light. Imposing looking statues and pillars lined the walls as if watching their every step.

"Where is Huur," Joe whispered looking around suspiciously.

"I don't know Joe, but I would be surprised if he didn't know we are here," replied Uncle Benedict.

Alert to possible attack, they made their way toward the center of the Pyramid.

The Gate stood in the ante chamber behind Huurs Temple. Fatima and Amal had found their way there through secret tunnels in the walls that Huur sometimes used and that only those with direct access to The System truly knew about. They were waiting to aid and abet the escape of the others.

The large Temple Hall stood empty as they entered through its magnificent golden doors. Large chandeliers lit with candles hung in the center of the room and their light flickered against the walls and floor casting shadows.

"Where now, Faras?" asked Joe.

Faras trotted cautiously toward the throne. She could sense the evil power that had been there. She moved over to the wall and there almost hidden, was the outline of a door. It opened suddenly and everyone flinched awaiting an attack but there instead stood Amal and Fatima.

Amal and Uncle Benedict stopped in their tracks.

"You, but how…" Amal spoke softly.

"Hello, Amal," replied Uncle Benedict.

"It's been so long, I can hardly believe it. But how?"

"That's a long story, for another time. I came to find you and free you but it looks like I was beaten to it. I guess I'll have to save Joe instead."

"Things don't always work out as we would like. If you have been helping Kareem and Aya then consider any debt you feel you owed, fulfilled. Though none of this was ever your doing."

Just at that moment a boom shuddered through the ground like the beginnings of an earthquake and the Gate began to shudder.

They all looked at one another.

Fatima closed her eyes and listened. "The girl has done it. She has succeeded in summonsing Nidar!"

"Quick," Amal cried, "you must leave now."

"But aren't you coming?" asked Joe.

"There is much to do here, if Aya has succeeded then we will have to rebuild this place. Please, you must go now."

And with that, Joe, Buster, Faras, and Uncle Benedict walked through the Gate just as the electrical shockwave hit and it disintegrated into a million pieces.

Outside, the chalk army fell to the ground like ash and the Dhegdheer's dropped into lifeless animals, electrocuted in their metal cases. Huur, though, had disappeared. He was nowhere to be seen, gone like a puff of smoke leaving Vincent standing alone on the balcony of a crushed empire.

The Warrior Faeries dusted themselves down and turned toward the Queen.

"The Ayannie has served us well. She was true," She announced proudly, to her people.

Nearing Huur's End

A tall, dark, stranger stood at the edge of the Barn looking out toward Ely Cathedral. "That fool, Vincent. That's what happens when you underestimate your enemy and think you are accomplices, Mister Vincent. Have fun in the other world! It's all yours," he cackled.

His body felt strange as he had shifted into it out of his bird-like form. It was not ideal but it was important not to draw attention to himself yet, until he was ready. These human bodies were so feeble, so frail. He was athletic and all powerful but he didn't feel it. He glanced down to find the earth a lot closer than he'd normally experience. A strange sensation coursed through him. It was vulnerability but he didn't know it, he felt weak. But here he was, on a new Earth, a planet he hadn't known but had always wanted as a dominion. With the knowledge gleaned by Vincent and the others, he could take over the Corporation and enslave the inhabitants as he had done with the Sectors. If these humans were anything like the ones he had just seen destroyed, it should be a very simple task. All he needed was money. For that was the currency they communicated in and on Earth and would commit any act of greed or violence for it. Picking up his bag, he sighed in contentment and set off for the Cathedral on the horizon, the largest citadel that could be seen and therefore the most prominent and important. Yes, all he needed was power and he would feel like himself once more.

As he walked through the lanes he began to tire but he continued on, not used to feeling fatigued. Many miles he walked until his stomach began to rumble. "What is this?" He had never experienced hunger before. A pleasant smell drifted into the air as he came across a shop.

"Food servant," he commanded in his most commanding voice at the woman behind the till, "bring me food!"

It was an old shop and had been serving the town for more time than most people of her generation remembered.

"Don't you come in 'ere making demands," Margaret replied. "You'll be civil or you'll get nothing."

Huur was confused. No one had spoken to him in that way before and it reminded him of his grandmother. He began to feel a wet trail coming from the corner of his eye and had a strange feeling in his stomach that wasn't hunger. He wanted to strike the woman down and send her to be tortured in the dungeon but he couldn't summons the energy and rage to make it happen.

"Where are my servants?" he blurted out angrily, looking around him for someone to take his anger out on.

"You'll be getting no servants in 'ere, my love, and if you don't act respectful I'll be throwing you out myself. Now what do you want. Make it sharp or you're out."

Huur stood in confusion of body and spirits before finding his voice. "I'm hungry," he said.

"Well, I got some meat pasties and a cheese and onion slice or sandwiches over there in the fridge. We got ploughman's, cheese and pickle or ham and mustard and you can 'av' a meal deal if you want to add crisps 'n' drink."

Confused and bewildered, Huur picked up his bag of money and opened it in front of Margaret. Surprised and alarmed, she looked into it. It was full of money, more than she had ever seen or would ever in her lifetime. Picking some notes up and looking closely, she replied, "It's foreign, we don't take that 'ere."

A strange howling noise, like an angry cry rang out over the town of Ely that sent birds flying from the trees.

Sad Partings, Reunions, and the End of a Journey

We stood together on the beach facing out to sea, watching the fleets of Warrior Faerie ships sailing into the distance.

"Do you think it will be alright?" Kareem asked.

I turned toward him, the breeze blowing my hair across my face. "I know it will," I replied, as we stood together under the setting sun.

"Thanks for everything," I said screwing up my nose. "I couldn't have done it without you."

"You definitely couldn't have done it without me," he said and we laughed together.

"What will you do now?" I asked.

"Try and return home, if it's possible. Sleep and wake up in your world, in our world. You know, just your ordinary, everyday activities. How about you?"

"I think the Gate is gone, that force field pretty much levelled everything. Return to a normal life I guess, eat cake, go fishing," I replied.

"Not save the world?"

"I've done that, bit exhausted now!" I said, smiling. "Be good to go to sleep without ending up in an adventure. At least I think that's how it goes. Who knows, I might be back here in a couple of hours. Fatima said she would try and help you return."

"I think your mum's waiting. I'm not good at goodbyes so, until we meet again!"

Kareem grinned a toothy smile and jumped up onto the Pegasus as it beat its magnificent wings and carried him away to join Fatima and the others.

She was sitting, waiting with her back to me watching one of the suns set over the ocean that had once been fire but was now an ocean of the purest blue sea water.

"Come and sit with me," she said without turning around, just patting the spot next to her with her hand. Tears streamed down my face as I sat beside her. She smiled at me and placed her arm around my shoulders as I rested my head against her.

"There child," she consoled. "I'm sorry about your friend Biriir." We sat like that for a long time, watched the sun setting and the stars begin to twinkle. We watched galaxies appear, bright as diamonds before us and shooting stars fly across the skies. The universe was indeed repairing itself.

"He had a giant heart," I said, "and now he's gone. I've lost him and I thought I'd lost you too."

"You never lost me. Biriir and I will always be here, in your heart, in your head."

"Mum, come back with me." I had to say those words but I knew it impossible.

"This is where I belong now, *habibti*. It can be such a beautiful life, a sad one, without you and your father, but there are many losses we must face in life and if we accept them, then it's OK. Treasure the happiness, remember it, keep it in your heart. You will feel it again, it is around you in every moment."

"That's what Dad says," I replied.

"That's why I married him," she smiled. "It filled my heart up with joy knowing that you were both out there somewhere in another world, laughing, dancing. Which one of those worlds do you think it might be?"

I looked over at the biggest planet, the most vibrant and said "hat one." We laughed together and though we could have spoken of a thousand things, it was not necessary and I fell asleep with my head resting against her.

I awoke to Buster licking my arm. Uncle Benedict and Joe were in the garden collecting walnuts and cherries and Joe ran to me when I walked outside. I swept him up in my arms and twirled him around. Faras had been munching on the goodies and was taking an after munchies siesta under the tree. We all cried upon seeing one another, hugged and jumped up and down with the excitement of it all.

"You've slept for a while," Uncle Benedict said. "We were a little worried but I thought it best you make your own way back."

"Yes, it was quite a journey. I wasn't sure, you know if I could do it."

"Speak with Nidar?"

"Yes, speak with her or even convince her. But in the end no convincing was necessary, she just knew, from me, from the people, from nature itself. She read what was happening and put it right."

"Did you get to see her in the end, your mother?"

"Yes. Just for a short time, but it was enough."

"And Kareem?"

"We must contact his father, Mr Shah. Fatima knows the ways of the Ancients and there may be a way for him to return. He lost Cube, of course, along with the destruction of the System. Meanwhile the others have a project, to help rebuild the planet and restore balance."

Joe said, "So is it all sorted now, all cleaned up, fresh and new?"

"Nidar removed the poisons in an instant but her powers are only to neutralize and eliminate. Regrowth and rebuilding the destruction of decades will take time. Mum is working together with Queen Qelhatat and the Warrior Faeries, they should be able to re-establish the beginnings of balance on sector C for Dameer and the other animals and perhaps the rivers and trees will be able to grow back once more and there will be more food and less sickness for the other forest creatures."

"And what about the Corporation?" Joe asked.

Uncle Benedict replied, "Vincent is trapped forever and gone into hiding on Moonlight. The Corporation has mysteriously lost its directors so their ability to impact on us is lessened, though I have contacted the man that will become the new director and I believe we have enough to threaten them with not to pursue further work on The Gate. Anyway, I have some new ideas about renewable energy that I think would be of far more interest and create greater wealth for the company."

"It's about time you got a job, Uncle Benedict," said Joe, dodging as Uncle Benedict tried to throw a cherry at him.

"Did we get *Moonlight* back?" I asked and we all weren't quite sure as we made our way down to the riverbank. And there she was, sitting in the water as though she'd never been away but coated in what looked like bits of stardust.

"Better contact your Dad and Jenny," Uncle Benedict suggested, "and we'll get some fish for dinner."

"Good job," I replied, "how long have we been away?"

"A couple of days," he replied.

"Feels like it's been years," I said, realizing just how much I appreciated my family and how much I was looking forward to being in my own room and having tea together.

It was a beautiful sunny afternoon in Ely with the breeze blowing through the barley fields. Jennifer had set out the picnic bench in the garden and I brought out the mini quiche we had made along with the blueberry muffins, tiny sandwiches, and Victoria sponge. Dad had insisted on showing Joe how to make samosas and there was flour and spice all over the kitchen. Buster had sneezed several times and gone off to snooze it off under the bushes in the shade. Faras had essentially moved in with the horses next to Uncle Benedict's field after the owners had gone away for the summer and he was now happily looking after them. We'd covered her in a horse coat and were planning on explaining that she'd been part of a circus troupe in Eastern Europe should anyone see her and ask questions and say that we'd rescued her. The roses were blooming, cream and pink and Jasmin flowered climbing in at the kitchen window which had brought all the bees out for a feast.

Uncle Benedict was fixing the lawn mower and at Jennifer's call we all congregated around the table.

"You two seem to be getting on better," Dad had said to me that morning. I thought of how I'd put Joe in danger, of how brilliant he had been on our adventure, and how frightened and protective I'd been when I thought he might become lost in the Dream World.

"He's my brother, isn't he," I replied, "got to look after him."

"So, how were your adventures out in the marshes?" Jennifer asked. She was still reeling from the huge hug I had given her on our return home. Me, Joe, and Uncle Benedict looked at one another.

"Just fishing," said Uncle Benedict.

"Picking nuts and fruit, you know, the usual," Joe said

"It was nice, but nothing much really happens in the Fens," I replied with a secret smile.

The clouds, like white candy floss, blew over a peaceful sky and then an announcement echoed through the air. A voice that sounded frighteningly familiar.

"You have now completed level 1."

We turned around to see a giant Cube appear above us, crystal white in the blue of the summer sky.

CPSIA information can be obtained
at www.ICGtesting.com
Printed in the USA
LVHW082005231022
731370LV00001B/195